THIS DIARY BELONGS TO:

Nikki J. Maxwell

PRIVATE & CONFIDENTIAL

If found, please return to ME for REWARD!

(NO SNOOPING ALLOWED!!!☹)

Rachel Renée Russell

DORK diaries

Tales from a NOT-SO- Talented Pop Star

548729
548729

THORNDIKE PRESS
A part of Gale, a Cengage Company

GALE
A Cengage Company

GALE
A Cengage Company

LIBRARY OF CONGRESS CIP DATA ON FILE.
CATALOGUING IN PUBLICATION FOR THIS BOOK
IS AVAILABLE FROM THE LIBRARY OF CONGRESS

ISBN-13: 978-1-4328-7476-6 (hardcover alk. paper)

Published in 2020 by arrangement with Aladdin, an imprint of Simon & Schuster Children's Publishing Division.

Printed in Mexico
Print Number: 01   Print Year: 2020

To my grandma, Lillie Grimmett.
Happy 90th birthday!
Thank you for a childhood stocked
with a never-ending supply of
pencils, paper, hugs, and dreams.

ACKNOWLEDGMENTS

To all my Dork Diaries fans — thank you for loving this book series as much as I do. Wow! Are we actually on Book 3 already?! Always remember to let your inner Dork shine through.

Liesa Abrams, my wonderful editor, who mysteriously seems to know Nikki Maxwell even better than I do. Thank you for making the countless hours we spend working on these books such a blast. And, yes, all of this happened just like you said it would. Go, Batgirl!

Lisa Vega, my magical art director, who never ceases to amaze me when she takes a single yellow sticky note and two simple colors and — ABRACADABRA! — turns it into a fabulous cover that practically flies off the shelves.

7

Mara Anastas, Bethany Buck, Paul Crichton, Carolyn Swerdloff, Matt Pantoliano, Katherine Devendorf, and the rest of my awesome team at Aladdin/ Simon & Schuster, thank you for all your hard work on this series.

Daniel Lazar, my super agent at Writers House, thank you for being there for me every step of the way. I could not have chosen a better "partner in crime"! And a special thanks to Stephen Barr for always making me smile.

Maja Nikolic, Cecilia de la Campa, and Angharad Kowal, my foreign rights agents at Writers House, thank you for taking Dork Diaries around the world.

Nikki Russell, my daughter and talented assistant artist, I cannot begin to thank you for all that you do. I am blessed to be sharing this dream with you.

Sydney James, Cori James, Presley James, Arianna Robinson, and Mikayla Robinson, my nieces, for being brutal critique partners and willing to work for a double cheese, double sausage pizza.

Sidney James, Gor James, Presley James,
Ariana Robinson, and Mikayla Robinson,
toy pieces. For being tried criteria, extra
pers and gilligan's work boss double
cheese, double sausage pizza

Friday, November 1

OMG!

I think yesterday was probably the BEST day of my entire life ☺!!

Not only did I have a FABTASTIC time at the Halloween dance with my crush, Brandon, but I think he might actually like me! SQUEEEEEEEEE!!!! ☺!!

By "like," I mean as a REALLY good friend.

Definitely NOT as a serious girlfriend or anything. I'm sure THAT would NEVER happen in a million years!

WHY? Mostly because I'm the biggest DORK in the entire school.

And with three zits, two left feet, one cruddy social life, and zero popularity, I'm not exactly the type of girl who'll one day be crowned prom queen.

But thanks to my wicked case of CRUSH-ITIS, the slightly-goofy-blissfully-lovesick-shabby-chic style I'm currently rockin' would definitely put me in the running for . . .

PRINCESS OF THE DORKS!

12

It's just that I'm NOT a tag hag (also known as a totally obsessed fashion SNOB).

And I'm NOT hopelessly addicted to spending twice the gross national product of a small third-world country on the latest designer clothes, shoes, jewelry, and handbags, only to REFUSE to wear the stuff one month later because it's "like, OMG! Practically more ANCIENT than YESTERDAY!!"

UNLIKE some people I know. . . .

"People" being shallow, self-centered girls like . . .

MACKENZIE HOLLISTER ☹!!

Calling MacKenzie a "mean girl" is an understatement. She's a RATTLESNAKE in pink plumping lip gloss and ankle boots.

But I'm NOT intimidated by her or anything. Like, how juvenile would THAT be?!

I constantly wonder how girls like MacKenzie always manage to be so . . . I don't know . . .

PERFECT.

I wish *I* had something that could magically transform ME into my perfect self.

It would have the amazing power of Cinderella's fairy godmother, be easy to use, and be small enough to fit inside a purse or backpack.

Something like, I dunno, maybe . . .
MAXWELL'S ENCHANTED LIP GLOSS ☺!

My special lip gloss would make each and every girl look as beautiful on the OUT-SIDE as she is on the INSIDE!

How COOL would THAT be?!

After spending hours studying the potential global impact of the Enchanted Lip Gloss phenomenon, I was shocked and amazed by my scientific findings:

Enchanted Lip Gloss does *NOT* look CUTE on EVERYONE! Too bad, MacKenzie ☺!!

Anyway, I really hope Brandon calls me today.

BEFORE
**ENCHANTED
LIP GLOSS**

(WE SEE A
NORMAL GIRL.)

AFTER →
**ENCHANTED
LIP GLOSS**

(WE MAGICALLY SEE
MY INNER BEAUTY.)

☺!!

← BEFORE
ENCHANTED
LIP GLOSS

(WE SEE A POPULAR
GIRL IN DESIGNER
CLOTHING.)

AFTER →
ENCHANTED
LIP GLOSS

(WE MAGICALLY SEE
HER INNER BEAUTY.)

I would totally FREAK if he actually did. But I'm pretty sure he probably won't. Which, BTW, brings me to this VERY important question. . . .

HOW ARE YOU SUPPOSED TO KNOW WHEN A GUY ACTUALLY LIKES YOU IF HE NEVER BOTHERS TO CALL???!!!

CRUSH IQ TEST: Carefully examine the following two pictures for sixty seconds. Can you spot the DIFFERENCE between them?

ANSWER: There is NO DIFFERENCE! These two dudes are IDENTICAL!

Which, unfortunately, means your crush basically IGNORES you whether he actually LIKES YOU or NOT!

CUTE CRUSH WHO ACTUALLY LIKES YOU

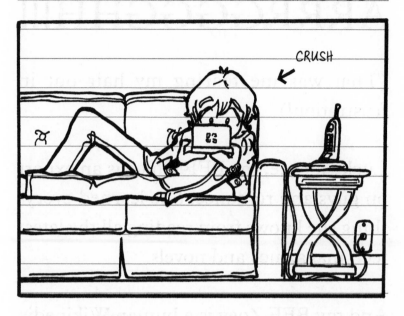

CUTE CRUSH WHO DOESN'T LIKE YOU

ARRRGGGGHH!!!

(That was me tearing my hair out in frustration!)

Lucky for me, my BFF Chloe is an expert on guys and romance. She learned everything she knows from reading all the latest teen magazines and novels.

And my BFF Zoey is a human Wikipedia and a self-help guru. She's basically a fourteen-year-old Dr. Phil in lip gloss and hoop earrings.

The three of us are going to meet at the mall tomorrow to shop for jeans. I can't wait to talk to them about all this guy stuff because, seriously, I don't have a CLUE!

Saturday, November 2

Can someone PLEASE tell me WHY my life is so horrifically PATHETIC ☹?!

Even when something *FINALLY* goes RIGHT, something else *ALWAYS* goes terribly WRONG!!!

My mom was supposed to be taking me to the mall today to hang out with Chloe and Zoey. So I was TOTALLY BUMMED when she told me I had to watch my bratty little six-year-old sister, Brianna, for forty-five minutes while she shopped for a new toaster ☹!

In spite of her cute little angelic face and pink sneakers, Brianna is actually a baby Tyrannosaurus rex. On STEROIDS!

21

There was no way I was going to hang out with my BFFs with HER tagging along.

So I told Chloe and Zoey I'd try to meet up with them as soon as my mom finished shopping.

I found a quiet, comfortable spot to chillax with my diary. Then I ordered Brianna to park her little butt right beside me on the bench and not move.

I hadn't taken my eyes off Brianna for more than a minute (or two or five) when I discovered she'd climbed into the mall fountain to hunt for coins!

Thank goodness that water was really shallow!

Then I made the mistake of ask- ing Brianna what the heck she was doing in that fountain. She put her hands on her hips and glared at me impatiently.

ME,
WATCHING BRIANNA
(SORT OF . . .)

"Can't you see it's an emergency?! A mean old witch has kidnapped Princess Sugar Plum. And Miss Penelope needs to get this money out of the water so we can buy a real, live baby unicorn from the grocery store and fly to save the princess!"

Hey, you ask a SILLY question, you get a SILLY answer!

I dragged her out of the fountain and made her toss back the big pile of coins she'd gathered.

Of course, Brianna was supermad at me for ruining her little treasure hunt.

So to distract her, I suggested we take a little stroll through the food court to try to find some FREE food samples to snack on. YUMMY!

That's when Brianna started nagging me to take her to her favorite kiddie pizza joint, Queasy Cheesy.

I don't have the slightest idea why little kids love that place so much. It has these huge, stuffed, robotic animals that dance and sing off-key.

Personally, I think it's supercreepy the way their eyes roll around in their heads and their mouths are always out of sync with their voices.

Maybe it's just me, but WHO would actually want to EAT in a restaurant that has a six-foot-tall, mangy-looking RAT scampering around? I don't care that it sings "Happy Birthday" and gives out free balloons!

To me, the ONLY thing SCARIER was that evil clown who used to live under my bed when I was really little.

My parents always insisted he was just a figment of my imagination. But he was VERY real to ME!

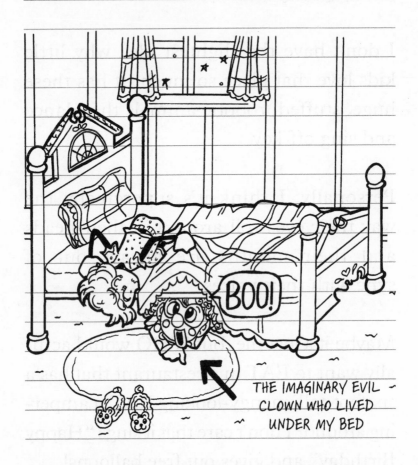

THE IMAGINARY EVIL CLOWN WHO LIVED UNDER MY BED

OMG! I was absolutely TERRIFIED he'd grab my ankles and pull me under my bed and I'd be STUCK there for, like, ETERNITY.

Thank goodness I'm older and more mature and NOT scared of silly, childish stuff like evil clowns.

Except maybe during thunderstorms on really dark nights when I see these strange shadows. . . .

Anyway! I was like, "Sorry, Brianna! I don't have any money. We'll have to wait until Mom gets back."

"But *I* can pay for it!" Brianna whined. "With my baby unicorn money from that magical fountain. I'm a RICH people practically! I wanna go to QUEASY CHEESY! NOW!!"

That's when I noticed that all of Brianna's pockets were stuffed with coins from that fountain.

My little sister WASN'T "a rich people practically."

But she DID have enough loose change to buy us a medium sausage pizza with drinks.

WOO-HOO!! ☺!!

The pizza was actually pretty good! For Queasy Cheesy, anyway.

Just as we were finishing up our meal, a waitress pulled a random number out of a bowl and excitedly announced that the guests at table 7 were the "lucky ducks" she'd selected to come up onstage and sing the "I Luv Queasy Cheesy" theme song.

I was like, "Oh, CRUD!!" Brianna and I were sitting at table 7 ☹!!

There was just NO WAY I was going up on that stage in front of all those people to sing that stupid song. And I made that fact VERY clear to the nice waitress lady.

Of course, that's when Brianna got an attitude about the whole thing.

She actually threw a hissy fit right there in the restaurant and — get this — REFUSED TO PAY FOR OUR FOOD!!!!

OMG!

I had never been SO embarrassed in my life!

Money?!
Well, you're NOT going to believe this, but
. . . BUT . . .

I totally panicked because all I had in my pocket was thirty-nine cents and some lint.

But the superSCARY part was that Brianna's silly little prank was going to land us BOTH in JAIL!

And YES! I'm aware that doing prison time is the latest fad for all those spoiled young celebs.

You know the type. The infamous party girl/model/actress who manages to become both an ICON and an EX-CON before her twenty-first birthday.

She truly believes she's above the law, because in her little mind the only REAL CRIMES against humanity are . . .

1. Fake designer purses
2. FRENEMIES
3. People with visible ear and nose hairs

So out of sheer desperation, I did what I had to do.

Namely, perform the "I Luv Queasy Cheesy" song with Brianna so she would pay for our meal.

Thank goodness the people there were mostly parents and little kids. I didn't see anyone I knew from my school.

Once we took the stage and I'd gotten past my feelings of extreme embarrassment and mild nausea (which is probably why they call the place QUEASY Cheesy!), I had to admit the whole experience was actually kind of FUN!!

The crowd seemed to love us, so Brianna and I really

HAMMED IT UP!

We were getting down with a few Beyoncé dance moves, and the audience was cheering us on.

Then the most AWFUL and SHOCKING thing happened. . . .

MACKENZIE HOLLISTER!

Apparently, she'd just arrived with HER little sister, Amanda, and her BFF, Jessica.

Jessica was pointing and laughing at me like I was the biggest joke since the interrupting cow.

And I totally FREAKED when I realized MacKenzie had her cell phone out and seemed to be taking a picture or something.

I grabbed Brianna and practically carried her off the stage.

"NOOO! Let go of me!" Brianna screamed. "The song isn't even over yet! We have to throw kisses to the crowd and —"

"Brianna! It's time to go!" I huffed, still out of breath. "Mom is probably waiting for us back at the fountain!"

But before we made it to the door, Amanda rushed over and shoved a pen and napkin into Brianna's hand. "I've NEVER met a real, live pop star before! Can I have your autograph?" she gushed.

Brianna beamed. "SURE! You can have it for FREE! And I'll draw a picture of my real, live baby unicorn too! I can ride him if I want. He flies in the air!"

Amanda's eyes widened to the size of saucers. "YOU have a REAL baby unicorn?! Can I see it?!"

I could NOT believe Brianna was lying like that. I gave her a dirty look and she stuck her tongue out at me.

"Well, I don't have one just YET. But I'm gonna buy it from the grocery store as soon as my mom comes back with our new toaster. 'Cause guess what?! Some idiot poured orange juice in our old one and it exploded and blew up our house. KABOOM!!"

"Brianna!" I scolded. "Move it! RIGHT NOW!!"

Actually, I was just trying to get out of there before MacKenzie came over. But no such luck.

"OMG!! Nikki! You were hilarious!" MacKenzie shrieked. "You stank worse than the boys' locker room!"

"Yeah, it took a lot of guts to get up there and humiliate yourself in front of the entire WORLD like that!" Jessica snorted.

I just rolled my eyes at both of them.

I knew I wasn't a professional singer or dancer, but the crowd seemed to like us. And since when had MacKenzie and Jessica become experts on talent?

"Oh, please! You two wouldn't recognize talent if it came up wearing a name tag, introduced itself, and slapped your face!" I blurted out.

MacKenzie and Jessica just glared at me. I think they were probably a little surprised because I usually just ignore them or say stuff inside my head that no one else can hear but me.

But there's only so much verbal abuse a person can take.

"And besides," I continued, "there aren't more than fifty people in here. I wouldn't call that the ENTIRE world."

"Well, it WILL BE when I post this on YouTube," MacKenzie said, sneering as she waved her camera right in my face. "Nikki Maxwell, LIVE at Queasy Cheesy!! And you can thank ME for launching your career as a NOT-so-talented pop star!"

Then MacKenzie and Jessica both laughed hysterically at her witty little joke.

I just stood there, stunned. Would MacKenzie actually do that to me?!

Something so . . . SINISTER and so . . . VILE?!

Suddenly my stomach felt really sick again and started making gurgling sounds like that angry chocolate fountain at MacKenzie's party.

Only it felt like I had just eaten a dirty gym sock and then washed it down with a large glass of room-temperature pickle juice.

If I didn't get out of there fast, MacKenzie and Jessica were going to have a SECOND video to post on YouTube. One of me BARFING stale pizza and watered-down fruit punch all over their $300 designer jeans!

When we finally met up with Mom, she was surprised I was so anxious to go home.

I just told her I didn't feel so well and had decided not to go shopping with Chloe and Zoey after all.

So now I'm in my bedroom writing about all this and trying not to

FREAK OUT!

Because if MacKenzie posts that Queasy Cheesy video on YouTube . . .

OMG!!!

Somebody please DIAL 911 because I'm going to have a massive heart attack and DIE!!

☹️!!

Sunday, November 3

I was so depressed about what happened at Queasy Cheesy yesterday, I could barely drag myself out of bed this morning.

So I figured . . . why bother?!

I decided to just lie there STARING at the wall and SULKING.

For some reason, wallowing in a truckload of self-pity always makes me feel a lot better ☺!

I finally got up around noon and spent the rest of the day online checking You-Tube. I was on there practically every ten minutes. I couldn't help it. It was like I was obsessed or something.

I was hoping MacKenzie had just been yanking my chain about posting that video.

She absolutely LOVES to torture me like that.

By 8:30 p.m. I'd come to the conclusion that the whole thing was just a nasty prank to FREAK me out. And it HAD!

MacKenzie is meaner than a junk-yard dog and totally despises me. But thank goodness she hadn't gone THAT far!

I decided to check one last time before I went to bed and then forget about the whole thing. . . .

It was official.

NIKKI MAXWELL, LIVE AT QUEASY CHEESY was now on YouTube for the world's viewing pleasure!

And it had already gotten seven views ☹!

I was DEVASTATED!

There was only one thing left for me to do. . . .

AAAAAAHHHHH!!!
(That was me screaming into my pillow!)

How am I going to face the kids at my school, knowing they're all secretly laughing at me behind my back?!

And what about Chloe, Zoey, and Brandon?

They're the greatest friends ever.

I cringed at the thought of putting them through more of the DRAMAFEST that is my life.

I kept repeating one thing over and over in my head. . . .

WHY ME?!

☹!!

Monday, November 4

There was NO WAY I was going to go to school today to face my public execution by video.

So I got up extra early to make a batch of my infamous Stay-Home-from-School Faux Vomit.

Unfortunately, that was NOT an option, because we were totally out of oatmeal. I was like, JUST GREAT ☹!!

When I finally arrived at school, I was expecting to be mercilessly teased, peppered with insults, and bombarded with a never-ending supply of very lame Queasy Cheesy jokes.

But to my surprise, no one even mentioned that stupid video. THANK

GOODNESS ☺!! Instead, the entire school was superexcited and buzzing about the upcoming annual Westchester Country Day talent show!

It's scheduled for Saturday, November 30, and the judge this year is Trevor Chase, the famous producer of the new hit TV show *15 Minutes of Fame.* Turns out he went to WCD!

The prizes were supposed to be pretty good, too, with first place being the chance to audition for a spot on his television show. How cool is THAT?!

So now Chloe, Zoey, and I are TOTALLY psyched about the talent show!

We've already agreed to perform together. We just have to figure out what we're going to do. It's gonna be a BLAST for sure ☺!

I'd give anything to be a rich and famous singing sensation!

WHY?

ME, AS A NOT-SO-TALENTED WCD LOSER

Because when Nikki Maxwell the WCD STUDENT is WEIRD, RUDE, SLOPPY, and CRAZY, everyone HATES her. She's called a LOSER ☹!

However, when Nikki Maxwell the POP STAR is WEIRD, RUDE, SLOPPY, and

ME, AS A NOT-SO-TALENTED

POP PRINCESS LEGEND

My hot dog is so groovy! *Burp!* But hold the mustard, please, 'cause I'd rather have my hot dog with peanut butter and cheese!

We ♥ You!

CRAZY, she gets mobbed by fans, paid millions of dollars, and everyone LOVES her. She's called a LEGEND ☺!

Anyway, I SAW BRANDON IN BIOLOGY TODAY!! SQUEEEEEEEEEEEE ☺!!

Well, actually, I see Brandon in biology *EVERY DAY.* But today was superspecial because it was the first time I've seen him since the DANCE!!

He told me (*AGAIN*) how much he enjoyed hanging out with me! SQUEEEEEEEEEEE ☺!!

And get this!! He said we should consider sitting together at lunch to study for our future biology tests!!! I blushed profusely and suggested that we start studying for the next test ASAP.

Like . . . TOMORROW! ☺!!

Mostly because I'm VERY serious about my studies. Especially my BIOLOGY tests!

ME, STUDIOUSLY STUDYING FOR ALL MY CLASSES AT THE SAME TIME!!

But Brandon said he couldn't sit with me at lunch for the next couple weeks because his editor has assigned him to train a new photographer for the school newspaper.

I smiled at him and was like, "Um . . . . Okay! Sure."

But deep down inside I was a little disappointed.

I started worrying that maybe he was just making up a lame excuse because he didn't want to hang out with me after all.

So I decided to talk to Chloe and Zoey about it.

Chloe said for me not to worry because Brandon was the one who came up with the whole sitting-together-at-lunch thing. Which meant he was ready to take our relationship to the next level. And Zoey totally agreed.

SQUEEEEEEE ☺!

OMG! I almost forgot! Now I have ONE more thing to lie awake nights worrying about. There were at least a dozen ants crawling around in biology today!

MacKenzie made a big fuss about getting ant germs until our teacher told her that if she didn't sit down and finish her lab report, her grade was going to be A LOT nastier than any ant germs.

But what if the problem gets worse?! This could turn into a major disaster! My teacher could complain to the janitor, the janitor could complain to the secretary, the secretary could complain to the principal, and the principal could complain to . . .

MY DAD,

THE SCHOOL

EXTERMINATOR ☹!!!

MUST. NOT. PANIC!! Breathe in, breathe out!

ANYWAY, before I so rudely interrupted myself, I was about to say that Chloe and Zoey think Brandon might actually like me!

And those little ants seem to think so TOO!

☺!!

TUESDAY, NOVEMBER 5

MacKenzie is even more EVIL than I imagined!

I was wondering why she had gone through the trouble of recording that video of me at Queasy Cheesy and posting it on YouTube, only to keep it a big SECRET!

It made no sense WHATSOEVER! But NOW I know why she did it.

I was at my locker jotting down ideas for the talent show when I was rudely interrupted.

"What's up, Nikki! I've got some super-EXCITING news to tell you, HON . . . !!"

I could NOT believe MacKenzie had the nerve to come up to me acting all friendly

like she hadn't just tried to DESTROY
MY LIFE a mere three days ago!

"I'm putting together a group for the talent
show, and I'm looking for supertalented
dancers with real star power. Here's all
the info."

Then she smiled really big, batted her superlong lashes, and shoved a piece of paper right in my face. . . .

I squinted and tried to read it.

But I was having a really hard time because she dangled it in front of my eyes and started swinging it back and forth.

And back and forth.

And back and forth.

Like she was trying to
HYPNOTIZE
me to do her

EVIL BIDDING
or something!

I knew right then and there she was up to no good.

It took every ounce of my strength NOT to be completely mesmerized by the brilliant radiance of her awesome, yet sickening, perfection.

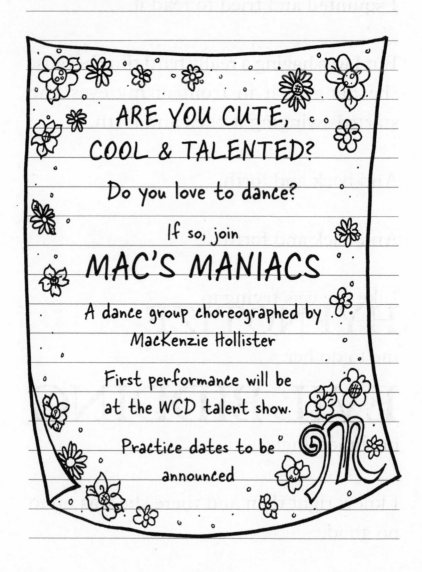

ARE YOU CUTE, COOL & TALENTED?

Do you love to dance?

If so, join

MAC'S MANIACS

A dance group choreographed by MacKenzie Hollister

First performance will be at the WCD talent show.

Practice dates to be announced

Finally I just snatched the paper from her and read it.

I had a REALLY bad feeling about that girl and her little dance-group thing.

Why in the heck would she want ME?!

Especially after Chloe, Zoey, and I got that D on our Ballet of the Zombies dance routine in gym.

Then there was that other small issue. . . .

SHE HATES MY GUTS!!

And after her very public and humiliating defeat at the art competition, I was sure she was hatching a diabolical plan to win the talent show.

Unless, after seeing me perform at Queasy Cheesy, MacKenzie had suddenly realized I was supertalented, with huge star power?

Maybe she wanted me ON her team so she wouldn't have to compete AGAINST me.

The whole concept kind of blew my mind.

That's when I started thinking that working with MacKenzie on her dance group might allow us to put aside our differences and *finally* become friends.

It would be nice NOT having to put up with her verbal abuse or worry about her blabbing my personal business.

I even tried to convince myself that hanging out with MacKenzie wouldn't be so bad.

Once I got used to her abrasive personality.

And her overinflated ego.

And her addiction to lip gloss.

And the fact that she has the IQ of a plastic houseplant.

I even imagined myself doing the kind of stuff I'd overheard the CCP (Cute, Cool & Popular) clique bragging about.

Like lounging on the beach at MacKenzie's summer home in the Hamptons.

I'd definitely invite my friends to MY summer home in the Hamptons! If I had one. . . .

Finally I made up my mind to give her a chance.

ME, IN A
SUPERCUTE SWIMSUIT,
LOUNGING ON THE
BEACH AT MACKENZIE'S
SUMMER HOME!!

Chloe, Zoey, and I were going to have a blast dancing onstage together in MacKenzie's group.

It would be just like our old Ballet of the Zombies days, only BETTER! I got a really warm and fuzzy feeling inside just thinking about it ☺!!

MacKenzie pulled out her new lip gloss, Decadent Dancing Diva Delight, applied a fresh layer, and stared at me with her icy blue eyes.

"So, Nikki . . . if you know any super-talented dancers with star power, like, um . . . CHLOE and ZOEY, just give 'em this flyer, okay?"

My brain was like, "What the . . . ?!! Did she just say 'Chloe and Zoey'?!"

Apparently, the little blond-haired wea-sel wanted ONLY Chloe and Zoey in her dance group and not ME!

Hey, I'd be the FIRST to admit that Chloe and Zoey were supertalented dancers, probably two of the best in the school.

But what did MacKenzie think I was? CHOPPED LIVER?! REFRIED BEANS?!!

It felt like she had just slapped me across the face. With a steel pipe or something.

"Um . . . sure," I muttered. "I'll tell Chloe and Zoey. But just so you know, the three of us were already planning on doing something for the talent show together."

"Well, you're going to have to CHANGE your PLANS, then! I really want that audition for *15 Minutes of Fame*. And if Chloe and Zoey perform with ME instead of a no-talent LOSER like YOU, it'll be a slam dunk for me to take first place."

I could NOT believe MacKenzie was talking smack right to my face like that.

"GIRL, PUH-LEEZE!" I said, doing one of those Tyra Banks neck-roll thingies that I'd practiced in the mirror for hours. "You must be delusional or something. Or maybe your barrettes are so tight, they're

MACKENZIE AS A PUPPETEER →

ZOEY

ME

CHLOE

cutting off the oxygen to your brain. In spite of what those voices in your head are telling you, we're NOT your little monsters! I suggest you go find some other people to be your puppets!"

MacKenzie was so angry, I thought she was going to whack me upside my head with her new Kate Spade hobo purse.

"I'm warning you, Maxwell!" she hissed. "If you so much as look at me the wrong way, I'll make sure everyone sees your little Queasy Cheesy video. You'll get laughed right out of this school. Even your pity-pals, Chloe, Zoey, and Brandon, will be too embarrassed to be seen with you!"

"This is a talent show, MacKenzie. Did it ever occur to you to try winning by using your . . . um . . . TALENT? Or is that a problem because you don't have any?"

MacKenzie took a step toward me and put her hands on her hips. "Better yet, maybe I'll just send out a text about your big secret. That you don't belong here, and your dad —"

"WHATEVER!" I shouted. "Like I really care what people think about me at this school!"

But I do care. And just the thought of her threats made me break into a cold, clammy sweat. My throat was so tight I could hardly breathe.

"Honestly, MacKenzie! The talent show is NOT that big of a deal to me and definitely isn't worth dealing with all your drama."

"Well, it's a big deal to ME! I DESERVE my fifteen minutes of fame, so stay out of my way."

Then MacKenzie smirked and flipped her hair in my face (like she was all that and a bag of chips) and wrinkled her perfect little nose at me.

"OMG! WHAT is that HORRIBLE smell?! I think the stench of your cheap perfume is starting to overpower my expensive designer fragrance. What did you spray on this morning, Macaroni and Cheese?!"

I just gritted my teeth and rolled my eyes at her. Is it a crime to eat mac and cheese for breakfast?! We were out of cereal!! ☹!

Then MacKenzie turned and sashayed down the hall. I just HATE it when she sashays!!

I was about to open my locker when I was practically trampled alive by a large group of CCP girls.

"OMG, MacKenzie! We just heard about your dance group!"

"Everyone knows you're going to win!"

"Mac's Maniacs ROCKS! Can I join?"

"Wait up, MacKenzie! Wait up!"

They scrambled after MacKenzie like mindless . . . lip-gloss-wearing . . . zombie . . . baby ducks or something.

I just stood there staring at the front of my locker like an IDIOT. I felt SO HUMILIATED!

Hot tears flooded my eyes and I tried my best to blink them away.

However, instead of crying, I decided to rip MacKenzie's flyer into a million little pieces.

At this point I want nothing WHATSOEVER to do with MacKenzie. Or that stupid talent show!

I'll be SO glad when this HORRIBLE day is over. ☹!!

Wednesday, November 6

I'm so sick and tired of MacKenzie manipulating me, I could

SCREAM!

I can't believe she's trying to keep me from competing in the talent show.

It's like she's OBSESSED with winning it. Her ego is SO BIG it has stretch marks!

I think the best thing for me to do is avoid her like the plague. Which is NOT going to be easy, because my locker is right next to hers.

I've decided that mentioning the video to my parents would just make things worse.

My mom would gush about how talented and ADORABLE Brianna and I were and would probably e-mail the darn thing to half a million people.

And of course, if I told Chloe and Zoey, the FIRST thing they'd want to do is watch it.

Which would be SUPERembarrassing!!!

And if Brandon saw it . . . OMG!!

He'd realize what a hopeless LOSER I am ☹!

NOTE TO SELF: Continue to check the video daily to monitor how many times it's been viewed.

As if things weren't already a hot mess, today was the second time this week I've seen bugs inside the school building.

I counted nine huge stinkbugs in the girls' locker room just while I was getting dressed after gym class.

One flew in my hair, and I totally

FREAKED!

← BUG

Of course, MacKenzie and the CCPs were practically rolling on the floor laughing at me.

Thank goodness Chloe and Zoey were there to help me. They are the best friends EVER!

As crazy as this may sound, BUGS are the very reason I'll NEVER, EVER fit in at this school. Mostly because I have a

DEEP, DARK SECRET!!

I only attend this fancy prep school because my dad arranged a scholarship for me as part of his BUG EXTERMINATION CONTRACT!

OMG!! I'm SO totally EMBARRASSED about it, I haven't even told Chloe and Zoey. Yet!

As a matter of fact, I've been at WCD for almost three months now, and not a single student here knows my secret.

Well, no one except . . . MACKENZIE HOLLISTER ☹!And she found out purely by accident.

One morning I was late for school and the only way I could get there was in my dad's work van. I've always been a little worried about riding with him because his van is old, needs a tune-up, and has a lot of things wrong with it — the most serious being the GINORMOUS roach sitting on top of it.

People stop right in their tracks and stare at it in awe.

Not only is it hideous-looking, but it makes you feel really . . . ODD.

Anyway, when Dad dropped me off at the front door of the school, I was superhappy and relieved that no one else was around to see me.

But then MacKenzie just unexpectedly POPPED OUT of nowhere. Like some kind of EVIL jack-in-the-box.

When I saw her standing there, I almost had a heart attack!

She was like this really big, ugly, infected pimple that had suddenly erupted right on the tip of the nose of . . . my LIFE!!

She stared at me with this shocked look on her face and said, "What is that hideous brown thing on top of your van . . . ?!"

I just rolled my eyes at her because, personally, I thought that was the STUPIDEST question ever.

It was OBVIOUS to anyone with a BRAIN that it was a roach, and it was up there on top of our van mainly to . . . um . . . do really important . . . stuff that was . . . um, actually NONE of MacKenzie's business!!

But the strange thing was that MacKenzie hadn't mentioned my dad again until yesterday.

And she's one of the biggest gossips in the entire school.

I've heard other kids gush that MacKenzie is so rich, she was born with a silver spoon in her mouth.

WAAAA!!!

SILVER ~~SPOON~~ SHOVEL

NOT!! MacKenzie's mouth is so big, she was born with a silver SHOVEL in it!

That girl CANNOT be trusted! ☹!!

THURSDAY, NOVEMBER 7

HELP!! It's only 7:30 a.m. and my day is already a

TOTAL DISASTER ☹!!

I'm beginning to think transferring to a new school might not be such a bad idea after all.

Which, BTW, would probably make MacKenzie

SUPERHAPPY!

I got up extra early this morning to finish my geometry homework.

I was just chilling out, eating a big bowl of delicious Fruity Pebbles cereal, and day-dreaming about BRANDON . . .

MY BRANDON DAY-
DREAM

ME

. . . when suddenly the telephone rang.

I had a really bad feeling about that call, even before I answered it.

Then, when I realized who it was, I just about had a heart attack right there on the spot!

WHAT I SAID: Hello . . .

ME ↓

WHAT HE SAID: Hi, this is Principal Winston. I'm calling for Maxwell's Bug Extermination. We've recently started having an insect problem at the school, and I'm a little concerned.

WHAT I SAID: *(GASP!)* Um . . . you've reached Maxwell's Bug Extermination. We're currently away from the phone. Please leave a message at the tone and we'll return your call. Um . . . BEEEEEEP!

PRINCIPAL WINSTON →

<u>WHAT HE SAID</u>: Yes, Principal Winston here, from Westchester Country Day Middle School. We need your services for a serious insect problem. Could you stop by my office tomorrow during school hours? I'll give you all the details when we meet. Thanks!

Still in a daze, I hung up the phone, grabbed my lucky pen, and filled out a message sheet for Dad:

FOR: **DAD**   URGENT ☒

DATE: **Thurs., Nov. 7ᵀᴴ** TIME: **7:15** AM/PM

WHILE YOU WERE OUT

FROM: **Principal Winston**

OF: **WCD Middle School**

PHONE: **You already have it**

AREA CODE   NUMBER   EXTENSION

TELEPHONED	☒	PLEASE CALL	
CAME TO SEE YOU		WILL CALL AGAIN	
RETURNED CALL		WANTS TO SEE YOU	☒

MESSAGE: **Needs you to come to WCD to discuss a bug problem. Stop by his office during school hours, Friday, Nov. 8th.**

SIGNED: **NIKKI** ☺

That's when the extreme AWFULNESS of the situation *FINALLY* started to sink in and

I TOTALLY LOST IT!

NOOOOO!!!

ME,
SCREAMING
IN HORROR

I was like,

OMG! OMG! OMG!

My principal wants my *DAD* to come to my

SCHOOL

to take care of the *BUG PROBLEM?!!*

My stomach got really icky like I had just eaten at Queasy Cheesy or something.

And I thought I was going to faint.

However, rather than waiting to DIE of embarrassment at school, I decided to take the initiative and end it all right then ☹!

By DROWNING myself ☹!

In my delicious bowl of Fruity Pebbles ☺!!!

I know it sounds like an INSANE idea. But I'd already tried it on Miss Penelope, my sister's hand puppet, and it had actually worked. Kind of.

ME, DESPERATELY TRYING TO DROWN MY SORROWS IN MY BOWL OF CEREAL!

However, in spite of my efforts, I ended up *STILL* very much ALIVE.

I felt so frustrated with my situation I wanted to SCREAM! Again.

Mostly because I had a half cup of soggy Fruity Pebble thingies stuck up my nose.

OMG! I must have sneezed Fruity Pebbles for, like, ten minutes straight.

They were plastered all over the walls and ceiling like rainbow-colored boogers or something.

I can't believe Principal Winston is expecting my dad to show up at his office tomorrow for a bug extermination appointment!!!

I'll TRANSFER SCHOOLS before I let my dad HUMILIATE me by DANCING around in his red jumpsuit (which, BTW, has MY last name plastered across the back), ZAPPING BUGS in front of the ENTIRE student body ☹!!

Everyone will think he forgot to take his meds or something.

I've officially designated my school as a . . .

NO-DAD ZONE!!

NO WAY AM I TELLING HIM ABOUT THAT PHONE MESSAGE!!

It just AIN'T gonna happen!!

After Dad misses that appointment, hopefully Principal Winston will just hire someone else to take care of the school's bugs.

I already HAVE the scholarship.

So what is Winston going to do? Suddenly just kick me out?! In the middle of the semester?! NOT!!

I think I'm going to wear my lucky socks tomorrow.

Hey, I'm gonna need all the help I can get.

☹!!

Friday, November 8

All day I've been a NERVOUS WRECK!

I felt superguilty about not giving my dad that telephone message.

But more than anything, I was

ABSOLUTELY TERRIFIED

I was going to see PRINCIPAL WINSTON in the halls.

I don't have anything against him personally. He's a little weird, yes. But so are MOST principals and teachers.

I mean, who wouldn't be TOTALLY INSANE after ten or fifteen years at a middle school?!!

Just hanging around this place as a STU-DENT for a couple of years can be psychologically damaging ☹!

Anyway, I was afraid Winston was going to mention something to me about my dad's appointment to exterminate bugs for the school.

That's when I decided it was superimportant for me to wear a very clever and cunning disguise so Winston wouldn't recognize me.

But unfortunately, I didn't have much to work with. Just my not-from-the-mall hoodie (with lint balls on it), a little imagination, and a lot of desperation. . . .

Not only was it brilliantly simple, but comfortable and FREE!

ME,
IN A VERY
CLEVER AND
CUNNING
← DISGUISE

Luckily, my disguise worked just as I'd planned ☺!

When Principal Winston saw me after French class, he couldn't tell I was actually ME! And he never mentioned my dad

98

or needing an exterminator, THANK
GOODNESS ☺!

He just looked a little freaked out. Probably because I was staring at him to test
my disguise.

Then Principal Winston did the strangest
thing.

He cleared his throat really loudly and told
me to skip my next class
and go STRAIGHT to

?!

WHAT
THE . . . ?!

ME
STARING

the office to get a four-hour pass to visit the guidance counselor!

At first I thought he was making a little joke or something.

But then I realized he ACTUALLY believed I was a seriously mentally ill WEIRDO!!

Now, how CRAZY is THAT?!

However, the good news was that I was getting out of four hours of class! SQUEEEEEEE ☺!!

Of course, I fixed my hoodie BEFORE I went to the guidance counselor's office. I didn't want HER to mistake me for a seriously mentally ill weirdo too.

We talked about how my classes were coming along and reviewed my new class schedule for next semester. Then after lunch she made me watch this superboring video series about career planning.

The four hours went by pretty quickly, and before I knew it, she handed me a pass to go back to class.

I really wanted to find Chloe and Zoey to tell them the exciting news about Principal Winston sending me to the guidance counselor.

But the school day was pretty much over, and it was time to go home. SQUEEEEEEE ☺!!

The very best part was that Principal Winston NEVER mentioned my dad! And my dad NEVER showed up for that appointment!

My flawless strategic planning, along with my very clever disguise, saved the day!

Am I NOT brilliant?!!

☺!!

SATURDAY, NOVEMBER 9

Today my mom came up with the stupid idea that we need to have "Family Sharing Time."

She patiently explained to us that "spending preplanned quality time together as a family would encourage love, mutual respect, and bonding."

I patiently explained to HER that she should STOP watching *Dr. Phil*.

Since we were stuck doing Family Sharing Time, I suggested we try one of those cool EXTREME SPORTS they show on MTV.

You know, the kind where you get to wear a helmet with cute designs on it, like hearts or rainbows.

So you'll look really cute when you break a leg or fracture your skull.

I think it would be fun, exciting, and educational if our family went BUNGEE JUMPING together ☺!

Okay, so maybe a family bungee-jumping trip is NOT such a good idea!

As expected, my parents complained that extreme sports were way too dangerous.

But that was a lame excuse, because Family Sharing Time can be ten times more DEADLY than all the extreme sports combined!

Like the activity they'd planned for today.

My parents excitedly announced at breakfast that we were going canoeing.

I almost choked on my waffle!

(It didn't have anything to do with the fact that we were going canoeing. I just eat really fast and tend to almost choke on my food on a regular basis.)

Anyway, my dad had purchased an old, beat-up canoe at a garage sale for $3.00.

He had his heart set on trying it out before winter sets in and all the lakes freeze over.

I was like, "Three dollars?! Dad, are you KA-RAY-ZEE?!! You spend more than that on your Egg McMuffin meal!"

But I just said that inside my head, so no one else heard it but me.

What IDIOT would risk taking his/her family out in deep water in a garage sale canoe that ONLY cost $3.00?!!

Okay, let me rephrase the question. . . .

What idiot . . . OTHER than my DAD?!
I love him and all, but sometimes
I REALLY worry about that guy!

Even a tiny, cheap, plastic pink
canoe for Brianna's doll costs MORE
than $3.00!

I'm just saying . . . !

The really scary part was that Dad knew
nothing whatsoever about canoes.

And since his was from a garage sale, it
didn't come with a manual, instruction
book, warranty, or ANYTHING!

When I mentioned my concerns, Dad
just rolled his eyes at me and said, "Hey! I
don't need to be a rocket doctor to locate
the ON/OFF switch."

DAD'S CANOE
$3

DOLL'S CANOE
$17

Anyway, Mom made PB and J sandwiches, Dad packed the car, and we headed out to this huge bay area that's really popular with boaters.

As I expected, the event quickly turned into a major DISASTER.

Mainly because Dad didn't figure out that a canoe required paddles until AFTER we got out on the water.

And then he got an attitude about the whole thing because HIS canoe didn't come with any paddles OR an ON/OFF switch (DUH!).

Which was probably WHY it only cost $3.00.

But I didn't bother to remind Dad of all that stuff, because he was kind of in a really bad mood.

So there we were, just floating around out on the bay for what seemed like FOREVER!

Thank goodness it was an unseasonably warm day or we could have gotten hypothermia or something.

Suddenly Dad's face lit up, and I knew he was getting another of his WACKY ideas.

He grabbed this large stick that was floating in the water. Then he took off his shirt, tied it to the stick, and let it flutter in the wind.

I guessed that he was trying to convert our paddle-less canoe into a sailboat or something.

But like most of his ideas, it didn't quite work the way he expected.

Whenever the wind blew, the canoe would just spin around in circles really fast like some kind of demonic amusement park ride.

Of course we were all a bit grumpy about our situation.

But thanks to Dad, now we were GRUMPY, DIZZY, and SEASICK ☹!

And Mom was starting to get on my LAST nerve!

Being the eternal optimist, she tried to cheer us up by making us sing "Row, Row, Row Your Boat"!

That's when I suddenly lost it and screamed, "Mom, has your reality check bounced?! Can't you see we don't have any PADDLES? How are we supposed to ROW, ROW, ROW the boat?!"

But I just said that inside my head, so no one else heard it but me.

And Brianna would NOT shut up! I had to restrain myself from trying to strangle her.

She was whining NONSTOP about the STUPIDEST things....

Okay, I love my family and everything. But sometimes I think they're, um...

A FEW CLOWNS SHORT OF A CIRCUS!!

Lucky for us, someone spotted Dad's homemade sail and assumed he was signaling for help.

Even though our Family Sharing Time activity got off to a really bad start, I have to admit it ended up being as exciting as any extreme sport.

WHY? Getting rescued by that Coast Guard helicopter was thrilling.

And being transported back to our car in that sleek, superfast police speedboat was a total RUSH!

When we finally got home, I was surprised to hear a phone message from Chloe and Zoey.

"Hey, Nikki, what's up? It's Chloe and Zoey here! We're calling to see if you're going to be available today or tomorrow to work on our act for the talent show. If so, give us a call. We can't wait to get started!"

I was like, Just great ☹! I really wanted to be in the talent show with them, but MacKenzie was going to make my life totally miserable if I did.

Sooner or later I was going to have to tell my BFFs I wouldn't be performing with them.

But I was so exhausted from our canoe trip, I just wanted to take a hot shower and crawl into my comfy bed.

I decided to tell them . . . LATER!

I wonder if Dad has figured out yet that canoes DON'T have ON/OFF switches . . . ?

Sunday, November 10

Mom and I are getting ready to go shopping to buy me some new clothes. I can hardly believe it!

I guess I owe Brianna a big thank-you since she's pretty much the person responsible for it.

It all started when Mom gave Brianna a new paint set and easel. She said it would help Brianna develop her artistic abilities.

So Brianna started painting, and Mom's been plastering her artwork all over the house.

The thing that really freaked me out, though, was this large portrait she drew of ME.

I couldn't believe Mom actually taped it up on our refrigerator like that.

What if a total stranger just randomly wandered into our house and saw Brianna's drawing up there?!

Hey, it could happen!!

But mostly that portrait was very damaging to my self-esteem.

I realize I'm not supercute like the girls in the CCP clique at my school. But PUH-LEEZE! Does my face *really* look like it got run over by a bus?!

And as if all that wasn't bad enough, Brianna is a very messy artist. She splatters paint EVERYWHERE!

I almost died when she actually got paint on my favorite shirt.

OMG! I had a hissy fit right there on the spot.

Okay, I'll admit it. That spot of paint on my shirt WAS kind of small.

But the last time I watched Judge Judy on television, she specifically stated, "Parents are responsible for the damage their child does to the property of other people. And that's the LAW, you @#$%& IDIOT!!" Or something like that.

Everyone knows Judge Judy is a very fair and impartial judge. She's also supergrumpy and possibly a little senile!

Of course, my mom took Brianna's side like she always does. She said, "Nikki, I'm sure it was an accident. I'll replace anything she gets paint on. Okay?"

I just looked at my mom and rolled my eyes.

"Yeah, right! And what if Brianna gets paint on ALL my clothes? Then you're going to buy me a whole new wardrobe?!" But I just said that inside my head, so no one else heard it but me.

Suddenly I had the most brilliant idea. That's when I decided to inspire Brianna's creativeness by finding stuff for her to paint.

I gave her my shirt to get started on. Then I ran upstairs to my room and tossed most of my clothes into a big laundry basket.

It felt really good helping my little sister develop her artistic skills.

Mom was really shocked when she discovered that Brianna had painted almost all my clothes.

Of course, I didn't tell her the part about it all being MY idea ☺!

Mom tried her best to weasel out of her promise to replace the clothes that Brianna got paint on. But I reminded her that as an impressionable young child, I was learning the importance of honesty, integrity, and keeping one's word from the example being set by my parents.

Which is the drivel I've picked up from all those TV talk shows.

Anyway, Mom felt SO guilty, she finally agreed to honor her promise.

Now I get to . . .

SHOP TILL I DROP!

SQUEEEEEEE ☺!!

BTW, I finally returned the call to both Chloe and Zoey.

I let them know that even though we weren't able to get together to practice over the weekend, we could meet to discuss our plans tomorrow in the library.

Which means I have to make a final decision tomorrow!!

What am I going to do???!!!

I'm so CONFUSED! I feel like my brain is going to EXPLODE!!

MONDAY, NOVEMBER 11

Every day during study hall, Chloe, Zoey, and I are excused to go work as library shelving assistants, or LSAs. We LOVE our job!

ME, CHLOE & ZOEY WORKING REALLY HARD PUTTING

AWAY LIBRARY BOOKS (WELL, SORT OF . . .)

After we finally got all the books reshelved, Zoey suggested that we decide what we were going to do for our talent show act.

That's when Chloe suddenly started doing what looked like the funky chicken.

Which meant she had just gotten a REALLY GREAT idea for the talent show.

"OMG! OMG! I just got the most FABULOUS idea! We can do a wicked cool dance routine about books. We'll call ourselves the BREAK-DANCING BOOKWORMS!" Chloe gushed.

"I LOVE IT! I LOVE IT!" Zoey squealed. "We can make fuzzy lime green costumes that look like caterpillars. And we can rap, too! What do you think, Nikki?"

I was like, "Actually, Chloe and Zoey, it sounds like a really fun idea. But is this supposed to be a TALENT show or a FREAK show?!"

But I just said that inside my head, so no one else heard it but me.

Chloe and Zoey are the BEST friends EVER! But they're also the second- and third-biggest dorks in the entire school.

So sometimes their ideas are a little . . .
how should I say it . . . DORKY too.

CHLOE & ZOEY'S WACKY IDEA #1,397:

BREAK-DANCING BOOKWORMS

But their occasionally weird antics are the
reason they are so much fun to hang out with.

I took a deep breath and tried my best to
break it to them gently.

"Actually, I think it's a really cute idea. But I have a bit of bad news. As much as I was looking forward to it, I've decided not to participate in the talent show this year. I'm trying to . . . um, spend more time on, um . . . schoolwork and stuff."

"Nikki! It's not going to be fun unless all three of us do this together!" Chloe groaned as her smile quickly faded.

Zoey looked disappointed too. "Well, if YOU'RE not going to be in the talent show, then I don't want to be in it!"

"Me neither!" Chloe said grimly.

"Come on, guys! You can be break-dancing bookworms TOGETHER. It'll STILL be fun!" I said, trying to sound upbeat.

But I couldn't get them to change their minds.

The three of us just sat there not saying anything for what seemed like FOREVER.

To make matters worse, I was starting to feel guilty about letting them down.

Finally Zoey broke the silence. "Nikki, are you mad at us or something?"

"WHAT are you talking about? Of course not!" I answered. "If anything, you two should be mad at me!"

"You've been kind of quiet lately. Is anything wrong?" Chloe asked, staring at me intently.

For a split second I thought about just pouring my heart out to them both.

About MacKenzie, Queasy Cheesy, the talent show, my dad, my scholarship . . .

EVERYTHING!

But instead, I shook my head vigorously and tried to muster a big smile.

"NO! Nothing's wrong! I just feel terrible that you guys have decided not to be in the talent show. I know you were really looking forward to it."

Chloe shrugged and looked out the window.

Zoey bit her lip and stared at the floor.

I reminded myself I was doing all this for their own good. The last thing I wanted was for THEM to be a casualty in MacKenzie's war against ME.

Finally the bell rang, ending fifth hour.

Chloe and Zoey looked sad and flustered. I think they knew I was hiding something.

And I felt just . . . AWFUL!

I sighed and tried to apologize. "Listen, I'm REALLY, REALLY sorry, okay?"

As Chloe and Zoey got up to leave, they both sadly muttered the exact same thing at the exact same time.

WHATEVER.

Then they turned and walked away ☹.

TUESDAY, NOVEMBER 12

I think I've finally figured out the source of the bug problem at our school!

I'm no expert (unlike my dad!), but it was kind of strange to see so many different bugs just randomly crawling around like that.

But here's the crazy part!

I accidentally left my French homework in my locker, and my teacher let me leave class to go get it. While I was at my locker, the halls were empty and totally quiet.

I could have sworn I heard CRICKETS CHIRPING!

And the sound was coming from
MACKENZIE'S LOCKER!!!

I was like, What the . . . !!

I stood on my tippy toes and tried to peek through the slot thingy at the top of MacKenzie's locker.

I thought I saw the silver lid of a jar or something, but her big leather purse was in the way.

That's when I got the brilliant idea to stick my ruler through the slot thingy to move stuff around and get a better look inside.

After a few tries I was able to push MacKenzie's purse out of the way.

And sure enough, right behind it was a glass jar. But I couldn't quite see if anything was inside it.

Using the ruler, I tried to scoot the jar toward the front so I could get a closer look.

But I somehow accidentally knocked it over, and it hit the locker door with a *KLUNK* and rolled on top of the purse.

That's when I noticed that the lid must not have been on very tight or something because it flipped right off.

I was like, OOPSIE! Time to get back to class!

But the longer I stood there thinking about it, the ANGRIER I got.

Mainly because it looked to me like MacKenzie had been secretly planting bugs all over the school.

She KNEW that sooner or later the school was going to call my dad to exterminate the place. And when it did, I was going to have a complete MELTDOWN.

There was NO WAY I was letting my dad come to my school.

I mean, what if he saw ME in the hallway between classes?!!

He might say something SUPERembarrassing to me like, "Hi there, Nikki . . . !"

Then, OMG!! I'd just keel over and . . .
DIE!!!

And from that day forward, I'd be known as the daughter of that crazy disco-dancing exterminator.

ME, THE HALF-BUG, HALF-DORK FREAK!

Kids would whisper stuff about me behind my back and call me a FREAK!

And not just a regular FREAK, but a half-BUG, half-DORK FREAK! Which is, like, ten times WORSE!!!

My life would be **TOTALLY RUINED!!** And it would all be **MACKENZIE'S FAULT** ☹!!

Unlike that talent show fiasco that involved my BFFs, this problem was just between ME and MACKENZIE. Which meant I could deal with HER on my OWN terms.

I marched straight down to Principal Winston's office to have a nice little chat with him about this bug issue.

Only, I didn't RAT out MacKenzie! YES, I know! I probably SHOULD have.

But I already knew from experience she was just going to bat her eyelashes all innocentlike and LIE THROUGH HER TEETH!

And Winston would totally believe her (and not me) because all adults think MacKenzie is a perfect little angel and INCAPABLE of lying.

Besides, I was going to talk to Winston about something WAY more important than MacKenzie's juvenile little pranks.

Our meeting went just as I had planned.

He told me he was happy I'd stopped by his office and asked how things were going as a new student.

I took a deep breath and got right to the point.

"Actually, Principal Winston, I'm doing fine considering the fact that I'm stuck with a locker right next to MacKenzie Hollister, and I'm totally lost in geometry. But I stopped by to let you know that since my dad is superbusy right now, you should just call in another exterminator. I'm really sure he appreciates your business and all, but there's only so much work he can handle."

Principal Winston blinked. Then he took off his glasses, folded his arms across his chest, and slowly nodded.

"Is that so? I was wondering why your dad missed our appointment on Friday. I thought maybe he didn't get the message I left on your answering machine. Well, it's quite a coincidence that you dropped by, Miss Maxwell, because I was planning to give him another call this afternoon."

"Well, if you want some advice, don't bother! He's so busy he hasn't even . . . slept in like, um . . . three or five days. Plus, it would be healthier for his . . . you know . . . sick gallbladder and stuff, if you just got someone else."

Principal Winston sat there staring at me with this really perplexed look on his face. Then I saw him glance at the telephone on his desk.

That's when I stood up, plastered a fake smile on my face, and shook his hand real friendlylike.

"Well, Principal Winston, I don't want to take up any more of your time. I know you're a busy man. Plus, I just heard the bell for lunch and I LOVE all the creative things your cooks do with mystery meat. I'm really, really glad we had this little chat."

"Thank you, Miss Maxwell. I'm glad we did too," he said, and cleared his throat.

Then I got the heck outta there!

As I headed down the hall toward the cafeteria, I felt like a huge burden had been lifted off my shoulders.

Winston was going to use another exterminator, and my secret would be safe again.

Problem solved!

As I got to the door of the cafeteria, a dozen CCP girls rushed past me screaming.

Inside, it was total

CHAOS!!

I immediately spotted MacKenzie standing on top of a lunch table shrieking hysterically and pointing at something lying on the floor in front of the salad bar.

My gut reaction was: Mouse?! Snake?!

But seeing as it was MacKenzie, it also could have been something as mundanely horrifying as a pair of red polyester pants. I have to admit, I wasn't all that surprised to see . . .

MACKENZIE'S BIG LEATHER PURSE!!

That's when I finally came to the conclusion that my earlier hunch was correct.

I guess there really WERE crickets in that jar! ☺!!

WEDNESDAY, NOVEMBER 13

The only thing everyone is talking about these days is that stupid talent show.

And it's really starting to get on my nerves!

People are practicing before school, after school, and even during lunch.

I'll be SO happy when all this is over!

I'd been waiting for MacKenzie to ask Chloe and Zoey to join her dance squad, so I wasn't surprised when she approached them about it after gym class today.

However, I was shocked when Chloe and Zoey turned her down!

They actually told her they didn't want to be in the talent show unless I was in it too.

I couldn't believe my BFFs had basically told MacKenzie to take her little dance group and flush it ☺!!

MacKenzie just stared at them with her mouth hanging open because she suddenly realized her plan to keep me out of the talent show had backfired.

She must have seen the smirk on my face because she gave me this really dirty look, and I was like, "WHAT?!" and batted my eyes all innocentlike.

I could NOT believe the disgusting, low-down, dirty thing MacKenzie did next.

"Okay, Chloe and Zoey. I'll be honest with you. Jason and Ryan have been BEGGING me to ask you to join. They're DYING to be your dance partners. I promised I wouldn't tell, but those guys

146

have really big crushes on you two!" she gushed, and then winked.

There was no doubt in my mind that MacKenzie was lying like a rug. She was only pretending to be Miss Matchmaker to trick Chloe and Zoey into joining.

But they believed every word she said and totally lost it. They started jumping up and down and squealing!

I didn't have the heart to tell them MacKenzie was a pathological liar and Jason and Ryan were probably in on her little scheme.

I shot MacKenzie a dirty look, and this time SHE batted her eyes at ME all innocentlike and said, "WHAT?!"

I was so mad I could SPIT! I wanted to slap that girl into tomorrow for playing with my friends' emotions like that.

147

Those two guys had taken cheerleaders to the Halloween dance two weeks ago and practically broken Chloe's and Zoey's hearts.

And NOW they were all going to be dance partners?!! I couldn't believe MacKenzie was such a little MANIPULATIVE . . . beady-eyed . . . SNAKE!!

What REALLY worried me, though, was the fact that neither Chloe nor Zoey had fully recovered from their totally debilitating case of . . .

CRUSH-ITIS ☹!!

MacKenzie was recklessly exposing Chloe and Zoey to yet another dangerous case of CRUSH-ITIS, merely for selfish gain. That girl is HEARTLESS!

So now they start dance practice tomorrow.

DR. NIKKI SHARES SOME GOOD NEWS!

"Well, girls! From your test results, it appears your severe case of crush—itis can be cured with medication."

DR. NIKKI SHARES SOME NOT-SO-GOOD NEWS!

"Unfortunately, you won't be able to sit down for a week. Now roll over, close your eyes, and count to ten."

I probably won't be seeing much of my BFFs over the next two weeks because they'll be hanging out with MacKenzie and the CCPs.

But it's not like I'm jealous or anything.

I mean, how juvenile would THAT be?!

☹!!

Thursday, November 14

OMG!!

I can't believe the
HORRIBLE
mess I've made!

I had no idea things were going to turn out like this.

WHAT am I going to do now?!

I think I'm going to be
SICK!

Which is the reason I asked my geometry teacher, Mrs. Sprague, if I could be excused to go to the bathroom.

ME

↓

ME, IN THE BATHROOM FEELING VERY WORRIED & SICK!!

Okay, this is what happened. . . .

When I got home from school yesterday, I stopped to get the mail.

I saw an envelope from WCD that was addressed to both me and my parents and figured it was my report card or something.

However, when I opened it, I had a heart attack right there on the spot because it was a TUITION BILL ☹!!

How did I know?

Mainly because it said in really big letters:

NIKKI MAXWELL TUITION BILL.

And below that was a dollar amount so big, I almost thought my eyeballs were going to rupture just looking at it.

I could try to pay it off with my teeny allowance. But that would take 1,829.7 years ☹!

At first I thought it was some kind of mistake!!

ME, TRYING TO READ MY TUITION BILL WITH MY ALMOST RUPTURED EYEBALLS!

But the only logical explanation is that I had messed up big time by NOT giving my dad that phone message from Principal Winston.

Then I had very STUPIDLY gone to Winston's office and told him my dad was too busy to come in. And now my scholarship has been revoked!!

WHAT was I thinking?!!! There's just no way my parents can afford to pay that tuition bill!

Suddenly it became very clear that MacKenzie had completely set me up!

Her master plan WASN'T to embarrass me by having my dad come to the school to exterminate all the bugs she was letting loose.

NUH-UH!! Her little brain was way more DEVIOUS than that!

Her plan was for my dad NOT to come to the school to exterminate all the bugs she was letting loose.

So I'd lose my SCHOLARSHIP and GET KICKED OUT OF SCHOOL!

She knew I'd be FRANTIC and do everything within my power to keep him away.

Basically, she TRICKED me into RUIN- ING MY OWN LIFE ☹!!

MacKenzie Hollister is an

EVIL GENIUS!

I had no scholarship and I had no money to pay the tuition.

My situation was **HOPELESS!**

As I sat there on that cold bathroom floor a thick cloud of anguish seemed to descend upon my stall like some kind of putrid smog, making it nearly impossible for me to breathe or think clearly.

Overcome by gut-wrenching emotion (and overwhelmed by that awful school bathroom smell), I began to ponder the unthinkable.

I wanted all my problems to go away.

So I decided to just end it all right there, by . . .

FLUSHING MYSELF DOWN THE TOILET ☹!!

But unfortunately, I was WAY too big to fit down that little drain-hole thingy.

That's when I noticed a bright yellow talent show poster taped on the stall door.

I'd seen them plastered around the school for days. But after all the drama with MacKenzie, I had never bothered to actually read one....

DO YOU SING, DANCE, OR HAVE SOME OTHER ENTERTAINING TALENT THAT YOU'D LIKE TO SHARE WITH THE WORLD?

IF SO, THEN COME PERFORM IN OUR 10TH ANNUAL
WCD TALENT SHOWCASE

Saturday, November 30, 7:30 p.m.

To be judged by TREVOR CHASE,

World-Famous Music Producer and WCD alumnus

PRIZES INCLUDE:

● Televised Audition on *15 MINUTES OF FAME*

● Scholarships to WCD

● Laptop Computer

● iPads

(and much more)

PARTICIPATION FORM MUST BE COMPLETED

AND TURNED IN BY FRIDAY, NOVEMBER 22.

(Noncompliance with rules will result in disqualification.)

See office for details.

I had to read that poster, like, three times before it finally sank in.

WCD was actually giving away

FULL SCHOLARSHIPS?!

I know I swore off the talent show earlier, but now things have changed.

I'm desperate.

How desperate am I?!

REALLY, REALLY, REALLY, REALLY, REALLY, REALLY, REALLY, REALLY, REALLY, REALLY, REALLY, REALLY, REALLY, REALLY, REALLY, REALLY

DESPERATE!!

☹!!

FRIDAY, NOVEMBER 15

Just when I thought my life COULDN'T get any WORSE, IT DID!!

I skipped lunch today because I wanted to talk to Brandon.

I really felt the need to vent to someone about all the stuff that was going wrong in my life right now, like for example . . .

EVERYTHING ☹!!!

Confiding in Chloe and Zoey was not an option since they were busy rehearsing with Jason and Ryan during lunch.

I still considered Brandon a good friend even though he's been so busy that we've barely spoken to each other since the dance two weeks ago.

It always seemed like talking to him helped me think things through more logically.

But most important, I wanted to tell him about my dad, my revoked scholarship, and that I might be leaving WCD very soon.

I'm just really tired of pretending everything is fine when it isn't!

And I know at some point MacKenzie is going to blab all my business to the entire school anyway.

Hey, world! My dad is a bug exterminator, and I attend WCD on a scholarship!

Big deal! It's WHO I really am!

WHY should I be ashamed of it?!

Even if MacKenzie has a problem with it, I don't have to.

Anyway, I rushed down to the newspaper office, since that's where Brandon has been hanging out lately training some new photographer.

Well, it looks like he's been pretty busy, all right. . . .

WITH MACKENZIE!!

I've always wondered if Brandon really likes me or not. Well, now I know.

HE DOESN'T!!!

I think he's just been using me all along to make MacKenzie jealous or something.

I couldn't stand to watch her gushing all over him like a lovesick puppy.

"Oh, Braaaaandon!" this and "Oh, Braaaaandon!" that.

OMG! She sounded so DITZY, I thought her brains were going to ooze out of her ears like syrup and make a puddle right on the floor.

She's more CRAZY about him than EVER!

And since WHEN has MacKenzie been into photography?!!

Probably since landing BRANDON as her
NEW TUTOR!

And get this! She doesn't even READ
our school newspaper, because she says

it doesn't have a Fashion & Style section. And the Fashion & Style section is the ONLY thing she says is worth reading in ANY newspaper.

The girl is DESPERATE!!

Anyway, I just turned around and walked right out of the room before they even saw me.

If Brandon wants MacKenzie, he can have her!!!

Saturday, November 16

My life is so MESSED UP!

All day I've been feeling SUPERdepressed and guilty.

I finally made the decision to come clean to my parents and tell them EVERYTHING!!

So what if I get grounded until my twenty-first birthday?

I was like, "Um, Mom and Dad, can I talk to you guys? It's really important!"

Mom was like, "Sure, honey. But can it wait a little bit? It's such a beautiful, clear night outside that your dad and I decided we'd all have a little Family Sharing Time."

I was like, OH, CRUD!! It was really BAD timing for Family Sharing Time ☹!!

Then Dad just about knocked me over rushing out the back door with a big can of lighter fluid and a box of matches.

Is it me, or do most fathers seem to have latent pyromaniac tendencies?

*DAD, WHEN SOMEONE ELSE IS
IN CHARGE OF LIGHTING THE FIRE*

HAPPY BIRTHDAY!!

They get really happy and excited whenever they grill food, light the fireplace, make a campfire, burn leaves, or do anything that involves fire. . . .

DAD, WHEN **HE** IS IN CHARGE OF
LIGHTING THE FIRE

What's up with THAT?!

Well, tonight Dad decided to build a campfire in the backyard so we could roast marshmallows. And Mom brought out a big plate of Hershey bars and a box of graham crackers so we could make yummy S'MORES.

I have to admit, I was actually looking forward to snarfing down that hot, gooey, chocolaty treat.

Sounds like a fun, family-friendly activity. Right?! It was.

Until Dad got a little carried away and burned his marshmallows to a crisp.

When they caught on fire, he totally panicked.

It looked like he was holding one of those flaming shish kebab thingies you see in fancy restaurants.

He was frantically whipping the stick around in circles trying to put out the fire.

The next thing we knew, those marshmallows were flying right off the end
of his stick and practically going into
orbit.

MY FAMILY, ROASTING MARSHMALLOWS

OMG! Dad's marshmallows lit up the night sky like a meteor shower or something. Actually, it looked kind of cool!

But somehow, in all the commotion, one of the flaming marshmallows landed on the front of his pant leg and stuck there. Of course Brianna totally lost it and started screaming her head off!

Thinking fast, Mom grabbed the bucket of water Dad had placed nearby and quickly doused the front of his pants just as it caught on fire. Thank goodness he wasn't hurt or anything.

But then our very nosy neighbor lady, Mrs. Wallabanger, came running outside to see what was going on.

Dad tried his best to explain to her that while he was out in the backyard roasting marshmallows, he'd had an unfortunate little accident.

Mrs. Wallabanger just stared at him with this really disgusted look on her face.

She gave Dad a lecture about how he should be ashamed of himself and actually threatened to call the police.

Then she stormed back into her house and slammed her door. But we could see her peeking out at us through her curtains.

We were all superconfused about why Mrs. Wallabanger was behaving so strangely.

Until I took a closer look at Dad and realized it actually looked like he had, um . . . wet his pants.

Which also pretty much explained why Mrs. Wallabanger had TOTALLY

FREAKED when Dad told her he'd had an "unfortunate little accident" in the backyard.

We finally decided to call it a night, and Dad put out our campfire by shoveling dirt on it.

Since Dad's pants were wet, dirty, marshmallow-covered, and slightly charred from the night's activities, Mom insisted that he take them off in the garage and throw them in the trash so he wouldn't make a mess in the house.

Then she rushed upstairs to get him a clean pair to put on.

Well, Mrs. Wallabanger must have STILL been pretty upset, because when Mom got back to the garage to give Dad his pants, we heard this loud commotion out in our driveway.

From what I could tell, Dad was having a really heated argument with someone.

It sounded like a lady was trying to convince him she was there to help him. But Dad kept insisting in a really loud voice that he didn't WANT or NEED any of her HELP.

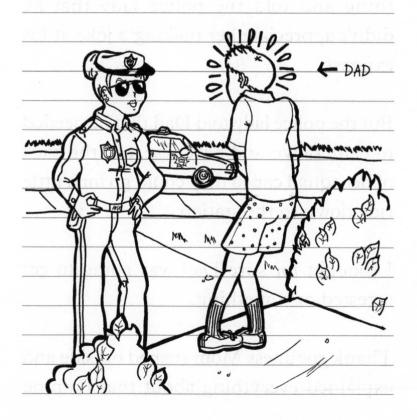

← DAD

That's when the lady said, "Actually, sir, I think you need to let me HELP you FIND YOUR PANTS!"

OMG! I was shocked to see that police officer! But I had to admit, she had a really good point about the pants issue.

Then Dad got an attitude about the whole thing and told the police lady that he didn't appreciate her making a joke at his expense.

But the police lady told Dad that he needed to calm down and have a seat in the back of her squad car so they could go for a little ride down to the station.

I thought for sure Dad was going to get arrested or something.

Thank goodness Mom rushed outside and explained everything about that flaming marshmallow, the bucket of water, and Dad's no-pants situation.

And after the nice officer lady was convinced Dad WASN'T wandering around the neighborhood peeping in neighbors' windows, she apologized to him and left.

In spite of the fact that the evening was a total disaster, Mom still insisted that we take a picture to put in her Family Sharing Time scrapbook.

So we all posed in the kitchen holding a graham cracker with fake smiles plastered on our faces, just to make her happy.

This was the WORST Family Sharing Time ever!

Since we were all pretty traumatized from the marshmallow roast and Dad was still

FURIOUS at that cop, I decided it was a VERY bad time to bring up the whole tuition bill issue.

Maybe I'll tell them tomorrow. Or I could always run away and join the circus. . . . ☹!!

SUNDAY, NOVEMBER 17

I was awake most of the night, tossing and turning and trying to figure out what to do about all my problems.

When I first started at WCD, I never thought in a million years I'd ever actually want to stay at this school.

But over the last couple months I guess the place has just sort of grown on me or something.

Chloe, Zoey, and I have become really good friends. I actually WON the avant-garde art competition. And then Brandon asked me to the Halloween dance. Although, thanks to MacKenzie, things aren't as good as they once were ☹.

All I really need to do is figure out how to fix it all.

At this point I basically have TWO choices:

1. Just give up and transfer to a new school. . . . Which means I'll ALSO have

OMG! LOOK AT HER CLOTHES!

LOSER!

to go through the TORTURE of being the NEW KID all over again ☹!

ME, AS A RUTHLESS CRIMINAL

2. Rob a bank and pay my tuition with the cash. Which, unfortunately, could be the first step in my new life as a ruthless felon.

Instead of spending four years in high school and four years at a major university, I'll spend eight years in prison for robbery.

And when I get married and have a baby, my poor daughter will take after ME and become a juvenile delinquent while she's still in diapers.

MY BABY'S FIRST ~~BIRTHDAY~~ FELONY

And then while I'm rotting in prison (and having superfun mani/pedi cell-block parties with those celebs), I'll realize what a horrible mess I've made of my life and totally regret that I DIDN'T give my dad that telephone message from Principal Winston!

Anyway, the ONLY choice I really have is to try to get a scholarship by winning that talent show.

Unfortunately, I'm just an okay singer. But if I was in a band with supertalented musicians, I might have a chance.

So on Monday I'm going to put up posters around the school and then hold auditions for a band. If I'm lucky, maybe there are a few really talented kids who HAVEN'T signed up for the show yet.

Monday, November 18

I arrived at school an hour early today to put up audition posters for my band.

I also got permission from the office to use the band room after school tomorrow.

I know this is last-minute. But all I really need is for three or four people to show up.

Although it was still fairly early in the morning, at least a half dozen groups were already practicing in various locations throughout the school.

The CCPs in the cafeteria were blasting their music so loudly I could barely hear myself think.

I peeked in and saw Chloe and Zoey dancing and flirting with Jason and Ryan. My BFFs looked SO happy.

There was no doubt in my mind that they'd enjoy dancing with Jason and Ryan more than being in my ragtag band.

ME, HANGING UP MY AUDITION POSTERS

I planned to tell them in the library today that I'd changed my mind about being in the talent show. I was sure they'd understand.

As soon as I got done with my posters, I rushed to class early to try to finish up some homework that I hadn't been able to complete over the weekend.

I can't believe how much homework they give you in middle school. There's just NO WAY you can get all of it done.

The last thing I needed was an incomplete, so I decided to come up with a really good excuse so my teacher would give me extra time to finish my assignment.

For some reason, teachers tend to believe stories that are really supercreative, no matter how crazy or far-fetched.

That's when I came up with the brilliant idea for a handy-dandy manual called:

THE STUDENT HANDBOOOK OF HOMEWORK EXCUSES FOR LAZY DUMMIES

I don't think there's anything like this on the market.

So I decided to write down all the best excuses I've used over the years and place them in a simple form.

And once I've collected enough of them, I plan to publish them as a book that could possibly become an overnight bestseller for students around the world:

FROM: _____
(YOUR NAME)

RE: Issue with My School Assignment

Dear_____,
(NAME OF TEACHER)

You probably won't believe this, but

☐ my spoiled sister

☐ my bratty brother

☐ my paranoid uncle

☐ my senile neighbor lady

has a pet

☐ snake, named Hubert,

☐ monkey, named Rocky,

☐ vampire bat, named Jean-Claude,

☐ unicorn, named Buttercup,

that unfortunately got really
- ☐ frightened
- ☐ angry
- ☐ confused
- ☐ sick

and unexpectedly
- ☐ projectile vomited on
- ☐ had babies on
- ☐ had a heart attack and died on
- ☐ had a really bad nosebleed on

my
- ☐ math problems.
- ☐ assignment.
- ☐ project.
- ☐ report.
- ☐ homework.
- ☐ _____.
  (FILL IN THE BLANK)

When I realized I would not be turning this
in to you on time, I became gravely depressed
and suffered uncontrollable

☐ sobbing.

☐ flatulence.

☐ hiccups.

☐ laughter.

I am truly very sorry for any inconvenience
this may have caused.

I assure you, it will NOT happen again

☐ EVER!

☐ until my next homework assignment is due.

☐ until the cow jumps over the moon.

☐ until the next exciting episode of
America's Next Top Model.

☐ (and if you believe this, I'd like to sell
you some ~~swamp~~ land in Florida).

Sincerely, _____
(YOUR SIGNATURE)

192

Hey! Maybe I can use the money from this book to pay my tuition ☺!

So, today in biology, Brandon was staring at me.

It wasn't like I was staring at HIM the entire hour or anything. I'm just very observant and happened to notice it.

I almost fell out of my chair when he leaned over and whispered, "Are you okay, Nikki? You look kind of down today."

But since talking to him would make me feel even MORE heartbroken than I already was, I just nodded and kept right on working on our human brain assignment.

Unlike MacKenzie! That girl would NOT shut up the entire hour!

OMG!

She babbled nonstop to Brandon about her new lip gloss flavors and Mac's Maniacs, all while making goo-goo eyes at him.

While observing MacKenzie's behavior, I prepared a lab report supporting my new hypothesis on intelligence and nutrition:

It IS actually humanly possible to have the IQ of a toaster pastry and still function in society!

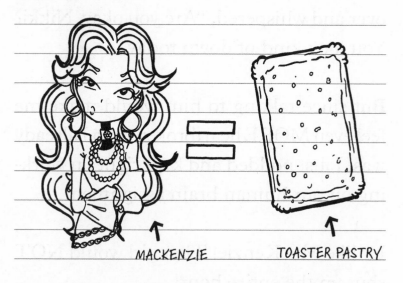

MACKENZIE   TOASTER PASTRY

Anyway, after class was over, Brandon didn't try to talk to me again or anything.

He just looked at me, shrugged, and walked away with this perplexed look on his face.

It's almost like he has no idea WHATSO-EVER why I'm acting the way I am.

Which is ironic because HE is the reason I'm a total PSYCHO.

How can he NOT know how I feel?!

But . . . what if he DOESN'T?!

What if he thinks I'm just being mean for no reason?

When I actually like him! A LOT!!

I think!

WHY am I so CONFUSED?!

☹!!

TUESDAY, NOVEMBER 19

Today was the BIG DAY! AUDITIONS!!

Although I felt superexcited, deep down I was really worried.

If I don't win the talent competition and snag a scholarship, I won't have any choice but to transfer to a new school.

Just thinking about it makes me break out in a cold sweat ☹!

And as if I wasn't already STRESSED OUT enough, MacKenzie kept staring at me and giving me the evil eye the entire time I was at my locker.

I was like, "Hey, girlfriend. You're creeping me out. Just take a picture, why don't cha?"

But I just said that inside my head, so no one else heard it but me.

All my classes bored me out of my skull, and the day seemed to drag on and on and on.

When school was FINALLY over, I hurried toward the band room to get ready for the auditions.

ME

As I passed the cafeteria, I couldn't help but notice MacKenzie and a few of her CCP dancers crowded around one of my audition flyers.

Of course when she saw me, she started whispering about me and giggling like an evil little witch.

She had a lot of nerve to be talking about me right to my face like that.

However, since I had somewhere to be, I just ignored her and rushed right past.

I got to the band room about ten minutes early and was relieved to see a dozen or so kids warming up on their instruments.

I started to feel a lot better. But mostly I was hopeful that maybe my crazy plan was actually going to work.

I could tell they were pretty good musicians just by listening to them.

At 3:45 sharp I decided to get the show on the road.

"Okay, I'm ready to get started now, if you guys are!" I said cheerfully. "Here's the sign-up sheet."

This kinda cute guy who was drumming on the seat of a chair looked up at me and smiled. "So, you're the one who's using the band room today? We'll be out of your hair in a minute. As soon as our tuba player shows up, we'll be moving to the choir room to practice with the glee club."

Out of my hair?! Now I was totally confused. I was pretty sure I must have heard him wrong. "Excuse me? Aren't you guys here for the talent show?"

"Yeah! We're the jazz band, and we're doing a few numbers with the glee club."

I just stared at him with my mouth dangling open. "Umm, okay. I just thought that . . . um . . . you all were here for . . ." My voice trailed off.

A guy rushed in and grabbed the tuba. Then everyone filed out of the room.

My heart sank. I groaned and collapsed into a chair.

Other than me, the room was now totally empty.

I glanced at the clock. It was 3:55.

Don't panic! I thought. *Maybe everyone is just late or something.*

I looked back at the clock and wondered if it had stopped working. It was moving so slooooooowly.

3:58. 4:00. 4:03.

And still no one arrived.

4:05. 4:08. 4:11.

By 4:15 I sighed deeply and finally admitted the obvious.

My brilliant plan was a complete and humongous

FLOP!

NOT a single person had bothered to show up for my auditions ☹!

I couldn't remember the last time I'd felt so alone.

I got a huge lump in my throat and tried
to fight back my tears.

I was such a LOSER!

Maybe transferring to another school wasn't such a bad idea after all.

It seemed VERY obvious that no one here actually liked me. I'd just been kidding myself to think so.

My thoughts were interrupted by Violet, who stormed into the room and slammed the door.

"Oh, there you are! What the HECK is going on? I told everyone they should have checked in here first! Some people are such IDIOTS!"

You ALWAYS know exactly how Violet feels about something.

Mainly because she'll tell you rather loudly whether you want to hear it or not. But I kind of like that about her.

"Well, thanks a lot for canceling your auditions at the last minute. I've been practicing that stupid song on the piano for hours! I guess fame eludes me yet again," she huffed, scowling at me.

I just shrugged and tried to wipe away my tears before she noticed them. "I'm really sorry. . . ."

Suddenly her face softened, and she looked concerned. "Hey! Are you okay?"

"Sure. Just, um . . . severe . . . allergies. Actually, I'm fine. But did you just say 'canceling'?!"

"Yeah! You did it on such short notice. What happened?"

"What do you mean, what happened?!"

"What do *YOU* mean, what do *I* mean?!" Violet looked at me like I was crazy. "You canceled it! Right? Okay, come look at this."

I followed Violet down the hall, and we stopped at the exact spot I'd seen MacKenzie and her friends almost an hour earlier.

Violet pointed at my flyer. "SEE? It says 'CANCELED'!"

Sure enough, scrawled across my audition flyer in black marker was the word "CANCELED!!"

I could NOT believe my eyes!

I rushed farther down the hall, to the flyer I'd posted over the drinking fountain.

It said "CANCELED!!"

I checked the flyer on the wall near my locker.

"CANCELED!!"

I went around the entire school ripping my "CANCELED!!" flyers off the walls.

Then I threw them all in the trash.

No wonder no one had bothered to show up for my auditions.

And I knew just who was behind it all.

MACKENZIE!!!

I could feel the tears coming again. Only this time they were tears of anger.

Since it was almost time for my mom to pick me up, I decided to take a short-cut through the cafeteria to get to my locker.

My mind was racing. I still had that tuition bill and no way of paying it.

What was I going to do now? Tell my parents? It looked like that was the ONLY answer.

As I entered the cafeteria, I suddenly heard music and familiar laughter.

I froze and gasped.

I had stumbled into MacKenzie's dance rehearsal. After what that girl had done to me, she was the LAST person I wanted to see.

I quickly slipped between two vending machines and prayed no one had spotted me. And from there I watched them practice.

I had to admit, MacKenzie and her group were really good. Especially Chloe and Zoey. As I had predicted, they were the best dancers by far.

That's when I realized my situation was hopeless. There was NO WAY I could win against her group.

As the song ended MacKenzie smiled at her dancers like a proud mother hen.

"Okay, everyone! That was FABULOUS! Let's take a ten-minute break."

Before I knew what was happening, the entire room came rushing in my direction.

Talk about CRAPPY luck!

There I was, trapped in a room with a bunch of hot, thirsty dancers.

And WHERE was I hiding? With the ice-cold sodas, juices, and bottled water, of course.

I was like, Way to go, Nikki!! My stupidity never ceases to amaze me!

I turned and tried to make a dash for the door. Only I forgot about TWO little things.

Well, actually . . . TWO very BIG things. . . .

I accidentally BUMPED into the first one and then TRIPPED and FELL over the second one.

And YES! Unfortunately for me, the garbage cans were still filled to the brim with very nasty, slimy stuff that students had either refused to eat for lunch or tossed.

And it smelled really, really . . . BAD!

Like slightly ROTTING . . . I don't even KNOW!

I hit the floor with a *THUD* and lay there stunned, covered from head to foot with disgusting garbage.

I felt like such a KLUTZ.

I didn't know which was more painfully bruised, my BUTT or my EGO.

But the worst part was that I had an audience.

Namely, EVERY CCP in the entire school! And of course, MacKenzie was in rare form.

"OMG, Nikki! WHAT are you doing in that garbage?! Scavenging for DINNER?"

Everyone was laughing so hard, they could barely breathe.

Well, everyone EXCEPT Chloe and Zoey.

"NIKKI! What happened?" Chloe gasped.

"OMG! Are you okay?!" Zoey asked frantically.

My two best friends each grabbed an arm and helped me to my feet. They were being SO sweet and kind to me, it almost made me cry!

MacKenzie reached into her pocket, unfolded a piece of paper, and waved it in front of my face tauntingly. It was one of my audition flyers.

"Sooo, how did your little auditions for the talent show go?! I see you chickened out and CANCELED it at the last minute," she said.

I couldn't believe she actually said that to me. I just stood there glaring at her as I pondered which was the fouler piece of garbage, MacKenzie or the reeking banana peel that was sliding down my forehead.

I was about to answer when both Chloe and Zoey turned and stared at me with surprised looks on their faces.

"Wait a minute. YOU'RE going to be in the talent show?!" Chloe asked, obviously shocked.

"I thought you said you didn't have time because of your classes and homework load?!" Zoey added. "Or is it that you just didn't want to be in the talent show with US?"

"OBVIOUSLY!" MacKenzie hissed, and handed them my audition flyer. "Looks to me like she'd rather hang out with who-ever wandered into her auditions than you two."

Chloe and Zoey looked very hurt.

I tried desperately to think up something to say to my BFFs.

"Actually, I, um . . . decided at the last minute and . . ."

MacKenzie quickly sized up the situation and went in for the KILL.

"Well, Chloe and Zoey, now you know what kind of BFF you have. As in, Best Fake Friend. Nikki OBVIOUSLY wanted nothing to do with you two. She doesn't deserve your friendship."

If there was an Academy Award for Best Actress in a BFF Breakup Scene, Mac-Kenzie would have won.

"OMG! I feel so SORRY for you two . . . !" She sniffed and blinked away phony tears.

Then she hugged them both like their puppy had just died.

"Chloe! Zoey! Please, please don't believe MacKenzie. I really wanted to be in the talent show with you guys. But a lot of stuff happened."

I couldn't believe how upset they were. They looked like they were going to cry.

". . . I was going to tell you about the band too. I just hadn't gotten the chance . . . yet!" I muttered.

"I've heard enough! Nikki is treating you like dirt. Come on, girls. We have a talent show to win!" MacKenzie grabbed Chloe and Zoey by their shoulders and led them away.

But before MacKenzie disappeared into the girls' bathroom, she flashed me an evil grin over her shoulder and mouthed . . .

LOO-ZER!

And right now I'm feeling like one. Because thanks to MacKenzie, my life has been totally

TRASHED!

No pun intended ☹!!

I've pretty much given up all hope of being in the talent show.

And I still don't have the slightest idea how I'm going to continue attending WCD.

When I saw Chloe and Zoey in gym today, I really wanted to apologize and try to explain everything before MacKenzie completely brainwashes them into believing all her lies.

But I never got a chance to talk to them because our gym teacher announced that we were going to be playing basketball.

Then she selected four captains to pick teams.

Unfortunately, I'm a very crummy basketball player and have NEVER made a basket in my entire life.

So I wasn't the least bit surprised when I was the very last person to be picked out of the entire class.

OMG! Talk about HUMILIATING ☹!!

And as if being the last person wasn't BAD enough, the four team captains got into a heated argument over who was going to get "stuck" with me on their team.

It's no wonder I struggle with low self-esteem!

I was hoping that Chloe, Zoey, and I would end up on the same team, but no such luck.

Anyway, the winning teams were going to earn an A while the losing teams had to take showers. This made me super-nervous because I HATE showering at school.

I never knew that playing basketball could be so . . .

PAINFUL!

And when I asked my gym teacher if I could wear a helmet, shoulder pads, and shin guards, she got an attitude about the whole thing and told me I just needed to hustle more and be a team player.

But what I really wanted to know was, HOW was I supposed to spend quality time writing in my diary when I was getting clobbered by that basketball every three seconds?!

By the end of the game I was sick of that ball. So when someone passed it to me,

I just whipped it right over my shoulder without looking. I wanted to get rid of it so I could write in my diary.

But get this! I made the winning basket with only two seconds left in the game.

Then everyone came running up to congratulate me! And my teammates hoisted me up on their shoulders like I was a hero and we had just won the state championship or something.

I had NEVER in my entire life seen people SO happy about NOT having to take a SHOWER!

While we were in the locker room, I was hoping to try to talk to Chloe and Zoey again.

But since their team had lost, they were stuck taking showers.

I quickly decided it would be more prudent to have a heart-to-heart with them at another time.

Besides, I just don't know what to say right now.

Other than the truth.

Which at this point is NOT an option.

Thursday, November 21

OMG! I could NOT believe what happened in social studies today!!

The cruddy thing about being so depressed is that I hadn't really paid a lot of attention to my homework assignment.

I mean, HOW can you study when your entire world as you know it is crumbling around you?

To make matters worse, class participation is an entire third of our grade.

So you CAN'T just sit in the back of the room texting all your friends about how the class is SO boring you're sitting in the back of the room texting all your friends.

Since I wanted to improve my grade, whenever there was a question I knew the answer to, I tried FRANTICALLY to get the teacher's attention.

TEACHER: "Is it really warm and stuffy in the classroom today, or is it just me?!"

Ooo! Ooo! I know! I know! PICK ME!

Hey! It was a QUESTION and I actually knew the ANSWER!

Of course, my teacher totally IGNORED me.

Like he always does when I know the answer.

Then we started discussing that social studies reading assignment that I'd ~~barely read~~ quickly skimmed.

TEACHER: "So, who can tell me how a democracy, a republic, a federal republic, and a parliament are different from one another, AND name a specific country as an example of each. Okay! Let's see . . ."

I tried to avoid eye contact and hide behind my book while chanting over and over in my head . . .

Don't pick me! Don't pick me! Don't pick me!

But did it work?! NUH-UH!

TEACHER: "How about . . . Miss Maxwell?"

Of course I looked like a total IDIOT because I didn't know the answers to his seventeen-part question ☹!!

That's when I totally lost it and screamed, "Um, excuuuuusse ME, Mr. Teacher Guy! But can I ask YOU a little question?! Why do you ONLY call on me when I DON'T know the answer? It seems a little DYSFUNCTIONAL or something, if you ask me!"

But I just said that inside my head, so no one else heard it but me.

When class was finally over, I was putting my books in my backpack when the strangest thing happened.

Violet came up and wanted to know if I was still going to put together a band for the talent show.

I just stared at her with my mouth wide open.

I could NOT believe she wanted to be in my band.

"Um, sure! I'd LOVE to have you on keyboard!" I said happily.

Violet smiled and gushed, "Thanks, Nikki. This is a dream come true!"

That's when Theodore turned around and gave me this really weird look.

Although, to be honest, Theodore ALWAYS looks a little weird. By some fluke of nature, he could easily pass as SpongeBob's human twin brother.

"DUDE! You're putting together a band?!" he asked excitedly.

"Actually, YEAH! I am. But isn't your band already signed up for the talent show?" I asked.

Theodore's band, SuperFreaks, had totally ROCKED our Halloween dance. And according to the latest gossip, they were an inside favorite to win the talent show.

"Haven't you heard? MacKenzie convinced most of my bandmates to quit and join her stupid dance group. She told them the cheerleaders had crushes on them and were dying to be their dance partners. Now there are only two SuperFreaks left — me and Marcus," Theodore said sadly as his eyes filled with tears. "The rest of our guys have gone . . . to the, the . . . D-D-DARK SIDE!"

He was so upset, I actually felt sorry for him. I gave him a tissue and he blew his nose.

"I'm really sorry to hear that," I said, trying to look very sympathetic that he'd lost the majority of his bandmates to the Dark Side.

Boy, did THAT sound familiar!

"So . . . um, do you guys need a bass and lead guitar player?" Theodore asked hopefully.

"The jobs are YOURS!" I said happily.

I explained to them both that I'd already made arrangements to use the band room for practices and that maybe we could have our first practice tomorrow morning.

And since the deadline for entering the talent show was ALSO tomorrow, I'd sign us up first thing in the morning.

"Cool!" said Violet.

"Yes! VERY cool!" Theodore added.

That's when it finally occurred to me that we still had a major problem.

"Um . . . the only remaining issue, guys, is that we need a drummer. We can't do this unless we have a drummer." I felt like a balloon that had just had all the air let out of it.

Violet looked crushed. "You're right! We won't stand a chance! CRUD! My music career is over even before it got started!"

Theodore squinted his eyes and tapped his chin like he was doing a really hard geometry problem in his head or something. "Well, like I said earlier, the SuperFreaks' drummer has gone to the Dark Side. But I know another guy I could ask. He said he was too busy to be in our band, but I'm thinking he might be willing to hang out with us just for a week or two for the talent show. He's really good, too."

"Really?!" I said, hopeful again. "Definitely ask him!"

I started thinking this crazy plan might actually work.

"Hey, we're IN IT to WIN IT!" I said, giving Violet and Theodore a high five.

"So, I'll see you both tomorrow morning, then!" I said as I grabbed my backpack and calmly walked out of the room.

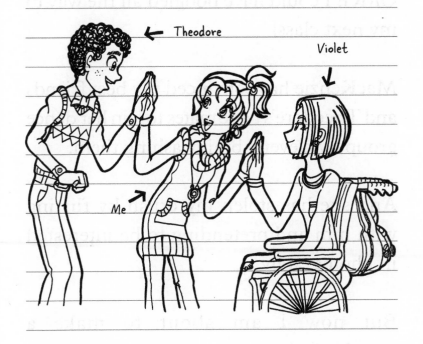

But inside my head I was SO happy, I was doing my Snoopy "happy dance."

OMG! I could have boogied all the way to my next class!

MacKenzie has convinced my best friends and Theodore's bandmates to join her dance group by cleverly brainwashing them.

And she has stolen my crush by flirting with him and pretending to be interested in photography.

But now I am about to make a comeback.

Starting today, I am going to put my time and energy into my new band.

And we are going to be FIERCE!

YEAH, BABY!!

☺!!

Friday, November 22

I was so excited about my first band rehearsal, I barely slept last night. I got up extra early, grabbed a granola bar for breakfast, and rushed right out the door.

Even though school didn't start for another hour and fifteen minutes, the halls were already noisy with ongoing practice sessions.

I was happy to see the main office was open, and I stopped in to fill out the paperwork to enter our band in the show.

Just as I was about to finish up, the LAST person I wanted to see walked in. Okay, make that the SECOND to LAST person.

With so much other stuff going on, I just didn't have the energy to deal with him right then. I tried my best to hide behind my backpack so he wouldn't see me.

ME, TRYING TO HIDE BEHIND MY BACKPACK ↓

BRANDON ↑

But it didn't work.

"Hey, you!" Brandon said with a big smile. He seemed pleasantly surprised to see me.

"What's up?" I answered, coolly noncha-lant. Like I HADN'T just been trying to figure out how to crawl into my backpack and zip myself up.

"Nothing much. I just stopped in to say hi to a friend," he answered.

I quickly glanced around the office. No students were in there except us.

"Well, no one has come in since I've been here . . . ," I said, trying to sound like I didn't care.

"Hey! Aren't YOU my friend?!" Brandon teased.

"Oh! You meant ME?! Sorry! I just thought . . ."

I bit my lip and blushed profusely as he stared at me with that look on his face. The one that can send me into a severe and debilitating case of RCS (Roller-Coaster Syndrome) in mere seconds.

I was like, "WHEEEEEEEEE!!" But I just said that inside my head, so no one else heard it but me.

I tried to regain my composure. "So, what are YOU doing here so early? Other than saying hi to a friend."

"Actually, I'm here for a talent show practice. I kind of got talked into it at the last minute."

I felt like someone had just dumped a gallon of ice water down my back.

Brandon?! In the talent show . . . ?!

Suddenly it occurred to me that if MacKenzie needed a dance partner,

HE'D definitely be her FIRST choice. I mean, why NOT?!

But HOW could Brandon just let MacKenzie wrap him around her little finger like that?!

"Oh, reeeally? How . . . quaint!" I said through my clenched teeth. "Sooo, I take it you're dancing with your little . . . Picture Pal."

Brandon blinked and looked slightly confused. "Picture Pal? I don't have a . . . Oh! You mean MacKenzie?"

DUH!!

I gave my best fake smile. "Yeah, I just hope you survive your BIG MAC attack!"

Then I very obviously rolled my eyes at the ceiling.

Brandon laughed, leaned over, and play-fully nudged me with his elbow. "Nikki, you KILL me! Big Mac attack?!"

Personally, I didn't see what was SO dang funny. "Yeah, you two have been inseparable lately. All that . . . PHOTO BONDING."

Brandon laughed even harder. WHY?! I was NOT trying to be funny!

Finally he glanced at his watch. "Well, I better get going. See you . . . later."

I couldn't control myself. It was like I had diarrhea of the mouth or some-thing. "Good luck with your Camera Cutie. I hope you both . . . um . . . break a leg!"

Brandon shook his head and gave me a weak smile. "Uh, thanks. I guess."

Then he turned and walked out of the office. I stared at him until he disappeared down the hall.

I replayed our conversation in my head.

Picture Pal? Big Mac attack? Photo bonding? Camera Cutie?

I cringed at my words. WHY did I always act so CRAZY and IRRATIONAL around that guy?!

No wonder he preferred hanging out with MacKenzie. He probably thought I was a NUT CASE!

I tried to put the two of them out of my mind. I had more important things to worry about, like band practice. Which, BTW, was supposed to officially start in two minutes.

I needed to finish the entry form and hand it in or we wouldn't be able to perform.

I had completed all the questions but one: NAME OF ACT?

Hmmm. We still needed to come up with a slightly edgy, cool-sounding name.

Something like . . . Purple . . . Poison . . . Fuzzballs . . . of . . . Doom? NOT!!

Or maybe Hungry . . . Plastic . . . Screaming . . . Toenails? NOT!!

So for the name of my band, I wrote in "Actually, I'm not really sure yet."

I handed the form to the secretary, grabbed my backpack, and rushed down the hall toward the band room.

I had no idea what to expect.

We barely had eight days to select a song and learn it well enough NOT to make complete FOOLS of ourselves.

Otherwise known as

MISSION: IMPOSSIBLE.

Theodore plays cello in the school orchestra, and his best friend, Marcus, plays violin. They are both "first chair," which means they are the best at their instruments.

I was really impressed how they had gone from playing classical music to Top 40 tunes. Although it probably wasn't that hard, considering the fact that the two of them have a combined IQ higher than the rest of the entire school.

These guys make ME (a self-proclaimed dork) seem like a social butterfly.

Their idea of a stimulating conversation is debating whether the *Star Wars* lightsaber or the *Star Trek* phaser is the more technologically advanced weapon.

Violet is pretty much a loner who spends hours and hours practicing classical piano pieces. I've heard she has played in competitions all over the nation and won.

But playing pop music on the keyboard is a whole different thing, and I was a little worried she'd make Bieber sound like Bach and Miley sound like Mozart.

Our biggest problem, however, was that we didn't have a drummer, and that really worried me. How could we have a good chance at winning without one?!

By the time I got to the band room, every-one was already there and warming up.

I was totally surprised to see the back of a guy stooped over, adjusting a drum set. Did we actually have a drummer??!!

Then he turned around and smiled and waved at me, and I practically FREAKED!

Theodore had recruited BRANDON?!

I didn't even know Brandon played the drums!

I just stood there like an idiot staring at him and then the other band members, and then at him and then the other band members, and then at him and then the other band members, and then at him again.

This went on for what seemed like FOREVER!

And then Brandon kind of shrugged and said, "Um, Nikki, are you okay?! You kinda look like you're having a seizure or something."

I was like, "Who, ME? Nothing's wrong! I mean, why would you think something's WRONG? I'm totally fine!"

But mostly I was in SHOCK because I could NOT believe that I FINALLY had my very own band and my CRUSH, Brandon, was actually there playing drums.

I was like,

"SQUEEEEE!!" ☺!!

Then we started talking about music, and I learned a lot of new stuff.

Like, musicians can play "by ear" or from sheet music.

The really supertalented ones can just listen to a song and figure out how to play it in a few minutes.

Otherwise, you can use sheet music and read the notes for the songs, which is a lot easier to do.

Well, guess what? My band is SO talented, they didn't even need sheet music!

I suggested the old-school song "Don't Stop Believin'," because it's one of my dad's favorites. I thought it was funny how everyone was into it again because it was on a TV show.

Each of them quickly figured out their own part, and within ten minutes they were playing it together.

It was absolutely AMAZING to see and hear!!

Then Theodore told me they were finally ready for me to sing along and handed me a microphone.

I was shaking so badly, I thought I was going to drop it.

Of course I muttered, "Testing, one, two, testing, one, two! Um, is this thing on?" like a total idiot.

It was on, and my voice was really loud and clear.

Just like the butterflies in my stomach.

After they played the intro to the song, I closed my eyes, took a deep breath, and started singing along.

We actually sounded really, really good. Well, really good for a band that had only been together for, like, thirty minutes.

When we finally finished the song, Theodore, Marcus, Brandon, and Violet raved about how well I sang, especially without having practiced or anything.

However, my little secret is that I've sung and danced to that song a million times.

In front of my mirror, using my hairbrush as a microphone.

The most surprising thing to me was that Brandon is SUCH an awesome drummer!

But he made me supernervous because he was, like, STARING at me the entire time.

I blushed and smiled at him. And then he blushed and smiled at me.

And when he thought I wasn't looking, he stared at me AGAIN!

So I blushed and smiled AGAIN! And he blushed and smiled too!

All of this staring, blushing, and smiling went on, like, FOREVER!!

Now I'm starting to wonder if Brandon actually likes me as MORE than just a friend!!

And if he DOES, I'll seriously just DROP DEAD from severe shock and extreme happiness!

I even wrote a poem about him.

Before I knew it, the hour had passed and it was time to leave for our first-hour class.

Since the talent show is next Saturday, we decided to practice one hour before school and one hour after school every day for the entire week.

Which means I'll be spending a lot of time with Brandon ☺!! SQUEEEEEE!!

DEATH BY DRUMMER
By Nikki Maxwell

Thump-thump!

Goes your bass drum.

Like the relentless

Pounding of my lovesick heart.

Rat-tat-tat!

Goes your snare drum.

Like fragile bullets of hope

Piercing the cloud of pure nothingness that is me.

Crash! Bang! Crash!

Goes your cymbal.

Like me very clumsily

Knocking over that row of folding chairs

Because you make me SO insanely nervous.

Does your skin sparkle in the sunlight?

Probably not!

But your intense eyes smother me

And your gentle smile fatally wounds

my jaded soul.

My heart skips a BEAT

and suddenly . . . STOPS!

Overwhelmed by the awesomeness that is YOU!

Give me liberty!

Or give me . . . DEATH by drummer!

Being in this talent show is one of the most exciting things I've ever done in my entire life.

I was really happy and in a supergood mood the rest of the day.

Even when I saw MacKenzie and Jessica whispering and giving me the evil eye during lunch.

I was like, WHATEVER!

My new band is beyond FABULOUS!!

And now I have a really good shot at winning that scholarship.

☺!!

WOO-HOO!!

Saturday, November 23

I planned to spend the entire evening brainstorming ideas for my band.

The show is less than one week away, and we still need to come up with a name, select a song, and figure out what we're going to wear.

Unfortunately, my parents announced that it was Family Movie Night and insisted that I come down and watch a rented movie with them.

My inner child screamed, "NOOOOOOOOO!!"

OMG! Talk about pure TORTURE!!

It's ALWAYS a SUPERold movie that's already been rerun a million times on

TV like *Raiders of the Lost Ark*, *Star Wars*, or *The Lord of the Rings*.

My dad says he loves renting them to see all the scenes that were cut out of the original movie release.

What he FAILS to realize is that the directors cut those scenes for one of two reasons.

Reason number one: They were BAD. And reason number two: They were BORING.

I was like, "Dad, are you kidding? Making us watch these movies for the seventh time is AWFUL enough. But we also have to see two additional hours of really BAD and BORING scenes. Personally, I'd rather get a big bowl of popcorn and watch the kitchen faucet drip."

But I just said that inside my head, so no one else heard it but me.

And my mom's favorites are oldies like *Honey, I Shrunk the Kids*; *Freaky Friday*; *Legally Blonde*; and *13 Going on 30*.

Which I HATE slightly less than Brianna's favorites: *Princess Sugar Plum Saves Baby Unicorn Island!* parts 1, 2, 3, 4, and 5. Princess Sugar Plum's voice sounds like a chipmunk on helium. . . .

"Please don't worry, all you cute, liddle, adorable baby unicorns. I, Princess Sugar Plum, am here to save you all! AGAIN! For the fifth time! All because I'm CUTE, LIDDLE, and ADORABLE, just like all of YOOOU!!"

Family Movie Night movies are SO LAME, I'd love to borrow Princess Sugar Plum's pink candy-cane magic wand and transport myself to the moon.

WHY?

SO IT WILL BE PHYSICALLY IMPOSSIBLE FOR MY PARENTS

TO FORCE ME
TO WATCH
THIS GARBAGE!!

That's why!!

I'm just saying . . . !!

☹!!

Sunday, November 24

Tonight my parents went out to dinner and asked me to babysit Brianna.

At first I was like, NO WAY ☹! But I finally agreed to do it after they offered to pay me.

I need the money to make some supercool T-shirts for all my bandmates.

We're going to look AWESOME wearing matching T-shirts with jeans when we perform in the talent show.

Am I NOT brilliant ☺?!

Anyway, the worst thing about babysitting Brianna is that she always takes TOTAL advantage of the situation.

And since I'm getting paid, she acts like I'm her little PLAYMATE-FOR-HIRE or something.

Which means for the past two hours I've valiantly suffered through a very

GAH!

off-key live performance of Brianna and Miss Penelope singing the hit "Single Ladies"! . . .

"Nikki, I'm gonna be Miss Penelope's backup singer when she goes on her world tour!"

AND I've attended a Princess Sugar Plum tea party dressed like someone's great-grandmother, with a doll and a motley crew of stuffed animals. . . .

You would think that after I suffered through these playtime indignities, Brianna would have appreciated it and NOT given me such a hard time at dinner.

But NOOOO!!

Mom left me specific instructions that Brianna could NOT leave the dinner table until she'd eaten ALL her broccoli.

So Brianna just sat there pouting and slapping her broccoli around on her plate with her fork like she was playing miniature golf or something.

I told Brianna she was going to have to either eat that stuff or sit there another forty-five minutes until her bedtime. Of course she got an attitude about the whole thing.

I left the table to put my dishes in the dishwasher.

And when I got back, I was shocked to see that Brianna's plate was completely clean and she had this angelic smile on her face that went from ear to ear.

You could practically see her halo.

I was more than a little suspicious.

"Brianna, are you SURE you ate all your broccoli?!"

She nodded and just kept smiling like an insane clown. But I was NOT about to be outsmarted by a six-year-old.

That's when I demanded that she open her mouth. Well, not HER mouth, exactly . . . Miss Penelope's mouth.

But surprisingly, Brianna had not stashed her broccoli in there.

So I gave her a big hug and told her how proud Mom was going to be of her.

She didn't say a word and just continued to smile like she was in a Miss America contest.

Unfortunately, NOW I know why!

I had tucked Brianna into bed for the night and was feeding the fish in Dad's aquarium when I spotted these strange chunks of green gunk floating around in the water.

At first I thought it was some kind of deadly, flesh-eating algae or something.

But upon closer examination it looked exactly like . . . Wait for it. . . . Wait for it. . . .

CHEWED-UP BROCCOLI!! UGGGHHHH!! OMG!

I almost lost my meat loaf right there on the living room carpet.

I screamed at the top of my lungs:

"BRIANNA! You SPIT broccoli in the fish tank?!!

Get down here and clean up this mess! RIGHT THIS MINUTE!!"

I was so MAD, I could have STRANGLED her!

I knew she was just pretending to be asleep.

Which meant *I* was the one STUCK cleaning *HER* slimy broccoli gunk out of the aquarium.

It was the GROSSEST thing EVER!

Babysitting that evil little munchkin is such a humongous PAIN!

As a matter of fact, the next time my parents ask me to watch her so they can go out to dinner, I'll pay *THEM* $30 to STAY HOME and ORDER a &!@#$% PIZZA!!

I'm just sayin'!

At least I have the money for our T-shirts.

All we need to do now is come up with a really cool name for the band and select our song.

☺!!

Monday, November 25

Today my

WORST
NIGHTMARE

came true ☹!

After an insanely boring morning at school, it was finally time for lunch.

I grabbed my lunch tray and was making my way over to table 9 when I noticed the strangest thing.

The ENTIRE cafeteria seemed to be staring at me and whispering and snickering.

At first I thought maybe toilet paper got stuck to my shoe from my trip to the bathroom.

Or maybe a humongous booger was dangling from my nose.

But then I spotted MacKenzie across the room, glaring at me all evil-like with this huge smirk on her face.

And right next to her were a bunch of CCPs crowded around her superexpensive hot pink designer notebook computer laughing their . . . um . . . behinds off.

That's when I got this really, really BAD feeling.

My thoughts were racing as I collapsed in my seat at the lunch table.

Could she have . . . ?!

Would she have . . . ?!

Did she DARE . . . ?!

Well, I finally got the answers to my burning questions when Matt looked at me and yelled . . .

Of course the whole cafeteria cracked up laughing.

My stomach was churning, and I had totally lost my appetite.

I kept thinking, OH. NO. SHE. DIDN'T!!

But MacKenzie HAD!!

I was SO humiliated! I blinked back my tears and tried to swallow the huge lump in my throat.

I wanted to run away, but at that moment I was too upset to move.

So I just stared at my tuna noodle casserole.

I was about to dump my tray and leave when MacKenzie sashayed over to my table.

"I heard you and some other DORKS from SuperFreaks started a new band. What are you calling yourselves, DORKALICIOUS?!"

"MacKenzie, why did you tell everyone about the Queasy Cheesy video?! I kept my part of the deal," I said, still fighting back tears.

"So what if you did! Now that Chloe and Zoey are on my team, I just have to make sure I don't have any major competition. And since I heard your little band was half decent, I figured now was the perfect time to let the world know what a talentless loser you are. SORRY about that!"

WHY in the world had I EVER trusted that girl?!

"Hey, Maxwell, I wanna see you do your Queasy Cheesy dance!" Matt continued to taunt me from the jock table.

"Matt, *I* wanna see *You* do some personal hygiene," someone retorted. I whipped my head around and was stunned to see Chloe and Zoey standing on the other side of the table. When had they gotten there?

Chloe slammed Matt with yet another insult as she slid into the seat to my left. "Dude, even your flies are starting to drop dead from the odor!"

"Yeah! You're SO nasty I wouldn't slap your face with somebody else's hand," Zoey huffed as she took the seat to my right.

I almost fell over from shock. It seemed like we hadn't sat together at lunch for ages.

"Are you okay?" Chloe asked, and gave my shoulder a squeeze. "We heard about that YouTube thing."

"We actually thought you and your sister were adorable!" Zoey said, smiling.

I didn't believe that "adorable" part for one minute.

I looked like a total idiot in that video. And it was VERY obvious that Chloe and Zoey were just lying through their teeth to try to make me feel better.

Which was one of the NICEST things they have ever done for me!

They are the sweetest BFFs EVER! I don't deserve friends like them.

I was just about to apologize to Chloe and Zoey and try to explain everything when MacKenzie started shrieking like a lunatic.

"Chloe! Zoey! WHAT are you two doing? I specifically instructed ALL my dancers to sit together at table four!!"

"Um, you guys don't have to sit with me. We can talk later, okay?" I muttered.

MacKenzie rolled her eyes at me. "Besides, Nikki is about as talented as a toilet plunger! OMG! That video was painful to watch."

"Well, at least I'm not a shallow, fashion-obsessed diva like you. If your brains were dynamite, you wouldn't have enough to blow your nose!" I shot back.

"OH, PUH-LEEZE! You're just jealous because you're not in MY dance group. Everyone knows we're going to win!"

MacKenzie spat. "Chloe! Zoey! It's either Nikki or ME! You better decide right now."

Slowly they both stood up. I felt HORRIBLE that they were choosing MacKenzie. But I really didn't blame them.

I was the biggest DORK in the school, and she was the biggest DIVA.

"Well, I'm glad to see you girls have finally come to your senses. At least you know a phony friend when you see one," MacKenzie said smugly.

"It wasn't a hard choice at all," Chloe said.

"I agree. There's so much phony baloney that if I had bread and mustard, I could make a sandwich!" Zoey exclaimed.

I just stared at my two friends. I felt like I had been kicked in the stomach.

Then Zoey placed her hands on her hips and took a step toward MacKenzie.

"We heard every word you said to Nikki. And you know what? You REALLY need to get over yourself! It's hard to breathe up in here with your stank attitude!"

I could NOT believe Zoey had just said that!

Chloe folded her arms and nodded.

"Yeah, I've had quite enough, *chica*. You can't treat our friend like that and get away with it. Oh, and one other thing. . . . I QUIT!!"

"ME TOO!" Zoey said.

"What?! You CAN'T quit!" MacKenzie screeched.

"WE JUST DID!" Zoey said.

"Yeah, what part of 'I quit' do you NOT understand?!" Chloe asked.

MacKenzie trembled with rage, and the water from the bottle in her clenched fist sprayed everywhere!

"FINE! I don't need you, anyway! Just stay out of my way, or you'll be sorry!" MacKenzie snarled. Then she stomped back to the CCP table.

I was SO happy my BFFs had chosen me over MacKenzie. And they had stood up for me too!

We did a group hug right there at table 9.

"Oh, well. I guess we won't be in the talent show after all," Zoey said.

"Yep! That's showbiz!" Chloe quipped, and gave us jazz hands.

"Hey, I have an idea!" I said. "Why don't you guys join our band? We're practicing after school today. We could use two more singers!"

"I don't know . . . ," Chloe said.

"Yeah," Zoey agreed, "I'm kind of sick of all the drama."

"Please!" I begged. "It would be just like our Ballet of the Zombies days! How FUN was that?!"

"Yeah! That WAS pretty awesome!" Chloe conceded.

"Even though we got a D," Zoey added wistfully.

"Well, before you say NO, at least come to our practice after school today," I pleaded.

"I guess that sounds fair," Chloe said.

287

"I can't wait to hear you guys!" Zoey gushed.

I could see MacKenzie staring at us from across the cafeteria and whispering to Jessica.

But none of that mattered.

I finally had my BFFs back!

☺!!

Tuesday, November 26

We had a BLAST at band practice yesterday!

Chloe and Zoey were superimpressed. And since they already knew everyone, they fit right in.

So now they're official members and will be dancing and singing backup ☺!

I can hardly believe my BFFs and I are actually going to perform onstage together.

SQUEEEEEEEEEEEEEEEEE ☺!!

MacKenzie's master plan to keep me out of the talent show had failed miserably. And now I was about to become her worst nightmare: stiff competition!

So it was poetic justice when we agreed to call our band **DORKALICIOUS** (courtesy of MacKenzie!).

We even wrote an original song that was inspired by MacKenzie's little insult.

It all started when Violet crossed her arms and smugly announced, "Hey! I'm a dork and PROUD of it!"

Then we started joking about which of us was the BIGGEST dork. The guys were like, "Can you please stop goofing around?"

Then Zoey said, "Actually, we're not goofing around. We're doing . . . um . . . vocal warm-ups."

"Yeah, and vocal warm-ups are VERY important!" Chloe added as she playfully gave the guys the stink eye.

That's when Zoey started singing, "Tryin' to fit in at my school, but kids keep telling me a dork ain't cool."

And Chloe sang, "Whenever the teasing gets vicious . . ."

"I remind myself I'm super DORKALI-CIOUS!" I chimed in.

We burst into giggles and gave each other high fives!

The guys just smirked and rolled their eyes at us. Then the three of them started whispering to one another.

I knew they were up to something, and I figured they were going to try to outdo us.

And I was right!

THEY started clowning around TOO!

The next thing we knew, they were dancing, singing, and frontin' like hard-core rappers:

> "Dork, nerd, geek, freak
> Is all you see
> But just back off
> And let me be ME!"

We all laughed so hard, our sides hurt.

The WEIRD thing was that their song had a catchy melody and a really great beat. It was the kind of song that gets stuck in your head for the entire day.

Even though it was supposed to be a joke, us girls actually LIKED it. Of course, the guys thought we were NUTZ!!!

But they finally agreed to let us try to turn it into a real song. While Violet, Theodore, Brandon, and Marcus worked on the music, Chloe, Zoey, and I quickly grabbed a piece of paper and finished writing the words.

By the end of our practice session, we had a very cool, original song about not fitting in at school, and being who you really are.

I have to admit, it isn't about superserious stuff like lost love or saving the world.

But it's OUR song, and it expresses how we feel. That's the most important thing.

Now that we finally have a name for our band, I was able to get started on our T-shirts.

Blasting my fave tunes, I threw a one-person paint-'n'-glitter party that lasted until midnight.

There is only one word to describe my
designer creation: "DORKALICIOUS" ☺!

WEDNESDAY, NOVEMBER 27

With everything that's been going on lately, I've been SO distracted. I'd probably

forget my head if it wasn't attached to my shoulders.

Everyone in the entire school seems to know about DORKALICIOUS!

Students have even started congregating outside the band room door to listen to us practice.

It's almost like we're a real band with real fans.

And NOT just a group of dorky friends who love music and have only been playing together for less than a week.

The latest gossip is that MacKenzie's dance group is no longer a slam dunk to win the talent show.

Which I guess is good news for us.

Especially for me, since winning the talent show scholarship is the ONLY way I can stay at this school.

I thought about telling Chloe and Zoey about my dad and everything else, but I think it'll just complicate matters.

The last thing I need is them questioning my true motives AND our friendship AGAIN.

But at the same time, keeping all these secrets feels really wrong.

ARRGGH ☹!! I have to ask myself:

WHAT WOULD SCOOBY DO?!!

Anyway, today is our last day of school before Thanksgiving break.

The dress rehearsal for the talent show is on Friday, and then Saturday is the big day.

PLEASE, PLEASE, PLEASE
let me win so I can get that scholarship!!

The good news is, even if I DON'T win, I probably WON'T have to worry about transferring to a new school.

WHY?

Because when my parents find out everything, they're going to KILL ME!

And it's probably ILLEGAL to transfer a DEAD BODY to a new school. . . .

Thursday, November 28

Today is THANKSGIVING DAY ☺!

I LOVE, LOVE, LOVE this holiday.

Mainly because I get to eat enough food to feed the entire cast of *Big Time Rush*.

Brianna and I helped Mom finish up the cooking while my dad drove to the airport to pick up my grandma.

Having Grandma over for the weekend is a real treat because we haven't seen her since we moved here last summer.

She said there was NO WAY she was going to miss seeing me sing in the talent show, and she was coming even if she had to ride her Segway the entire three hundred miles.

GRANDMA

And she's CRAZY enough to do it!

Grandma says all her friends have Segways too. And for fun, they get together and ride around town like an elderly motorcycle gang swigging bottles of Pepto-Bismol and squirting denture cream on the door handles of parked cars.

Grandma's a little wacky! Actually . . . A LOT wacky!

But Mom says that's because she has an eccentric personality and a zest for life. Personally, I think all that's just a polite way of saying she's SENILE.

But you GOTTA LOVE HER ☺!!

Here she is with her three adorable poodles named Larry, Moe, and Curly.

GRANDMA →

Anyway, our Thanksgiving dinner was WONDERFUL!

GRANDMA

After everyone had stuffed themselves, Dad lit the fireplace in our living room and we all sat around and played a game of charades.

It was my brilliant idea to do famous singers, and we took turns drawing names out of a hat.

When it was Grandma's turn, we almost DIED laughing.

OMG! She did a KILLER impression of Lady Gaga!

After our game was over, Grandma gathered us around and hugged each one of us. Her eyes started to water as she announced that she had something really important to say.

"I guess I should tell you the real reason I wanted to spend Thanksgiving here. I'm getting up in age, and one day soon I'm going to be leaving here and going on a VERY long trip. I know we're going to miss each other, but I want everyone

to know how much I love you all. So I'm
giving you your Christmas present today.

Mainly because I'm NOT going to be here with you physically for the upcoming holidays. But I WILL be here in spirit!"

That's when Dad got really emotional, and tears started streaming down his face. "Mom, we love you, too. But please don't talk about dying and leaving us!"

OMG! It was SO sad, even I sniffed a couple of times.

That's when Grandma turned around in her chair and rolled her eyes at my dad like he was a COMPLETE IDIOT.

"For Pete's sake! When you were a baby, your dad must have dropped you on your head a few times too many. Who's talking about DYING?! Gladys, Beatrice, and I are flying out to Las Vegas for two weeks, and we're leaving next Wednesday. From there we're doing a road trip to Hollywood

to see a taping of Betty White's show and
The Price Is Right! We won't be back until
AFTER Christmas."

We all breathed a HUGE sigh of relief.

Grandma continued, "Anyway, before I leave, I want to give you all an early Christmas present! It's a priceless family heirloom that has been passed down through generations of Maxwells since 1894. Or was it 1984? One of those years. I forget which. Anyway, it's my most prized possession."

She went to the closet and pulled out a large Christmas present topped with a shiny red bow.

That's when it occurred to me that if her heirloom was a superexpensive antique, maybe my parents could sell it on eBay, use MY portion to pay off my tuition, and STILL have thousands of dollars left over.

Maybe Grandma coming to visit and giving us our present a month early was the answer to my prayer.

NOT!

When we opened the box, inside was a SUPERold iron bucket with a large handle on the side.

My dad's eyes lit up and then quickly filled with tears again.

"MOM, you shouldn't have!!" he gasped. "It's Grandma Gertrude's ice cream maker. She used to make me ice cream with it when I was a little boy!"

I was like, JUST GREAT! So much for my idea of selling it to pay my tuition bill ☹!

Our so-called priceless heirloom was basically a piece of JUNK!

By next month we'd probably be using it as a makeshift recycling bin. Then during our annual spring cleaning Mom would pay the junk hauler to take it and a few other of Dad's garage sale treasures (like his paddle-less canoe) to the city dump.

Grandma handed my mom a piece of paper that had the Maxwells' secret ice cream recipe written on it.

"I'd LOVE some creamy, delicious, Maxwell family ice cream for dessert. Anyone else?" Grandma beamed proudly.

Brianna got so excited, she started dancing around. "Yaaay! I scream! You scream! We all scream for ICE CREAM!"

"What a great idea!!" Mom said as she herded us all into the kitchen. "I think making ice cream together would be a wonderful Family Sharing Time! Come on, everyone. FUN, FUN, FUN!"

I was like, oh crud! Family Sharing Time? Again? Nooooooo! ☹!

Making homemade ice cream sounds like a harmless, family-friendly activity. Right?

But NOT with an antique, cast-iron, hand-cranked ice cream maker.

Things got REALLY complicated when Dad showed Brianna what he used to do for fun when he was her age.

When Mom wasn't looking, he and Brianna tried to SNEAK a few licks of ice cream that had spilled over the sides.

Who'd have thunk such an old-fashioned gadget like that could reach FUTURISTIC SUBZERO TEMPERATURES?!

Can you find the TWO things very WRONG with this picture?! I'm just sayin' . . . !!

THE MAXWELL FAMILY
MAKING HOMEMADE ICE CREAM

AAAAHHH!

HALP! I think my thung iz thuck on da thide of thiz iceth keam thingy!!

After this little fiasco, I now know for certain who Brianna inherited her LACK of intelligence from!

I thought for sure their tongues were going to freeze solid, snap off, fall on the floor, and shatter into a million little pieces.

Luckily, Dad and Brianna only ended up with a mild case of frostbite. And a severe, but temporary, lisp.

I was surprised Mom's ice cream was so DELISH!

But every time that image of Dad and Brianna popped into my head, I'd start laughing so hard that ice cream would shoot right out of my nose and give me a really painful BRAIN FREEZE.

Hey, I wonder if it's true that if you take a hot shower right after a brain freeze, your brain will melt and you'll turn into a CCP. Hmmmm . . .

Anyway, we had a very HAPPY THANKSGIVING!

☺!!

Friday, November 29

Today was the talent show rehearsal at the WCD High School auditorium.

It's a fairly new facility that seats two thousand people. Just the thought of performing in front of such a large crowd gave me butterflies.

The guys set up all our equipment while Chloe, Zoey, and I did vocal warm-ups.

Violet hung out with us too and kept telling us how great we sounded.

The high school student producer of the talent show was Sasha Ambrose, a super-talented senior who won the competition two years straight when she was in middle school.

The butterflies in my stomach were quickly replaced by a cold, heavy lump of dread when I saw MacKenzie backstage, whispering to Sasha and pointing at ME ☹!

All the talent gathered in the auditorium and waited excitedly for Sasha to assign dressing rooms and give us our order of performance.

There was a total of eighteen acts, and she called them up one by one, EXCEPT Dorkalicious.

After all the others were dismissed to go backstage, she finally motioned for us to have a seat in the front row.

Of course we were all concerned about why we hadn't been called up along with the others.

Sasha pulled out our entry form, read it over, and slowly shook her head. "So, what's the name of your group?"

"Dorkalicious!" we all answered at once.

"Well, unfortunately, I have some bad news. It's been brought to my attention that the deadline for all entry forms was Friday, November twenty-second. And it specifically states here in writing that failure to submit a completed form will result in disqualification from the show."

I didn't have the slightest idea why she was telling us all of this.

I had *personally* completed our entry form right there in the school office and handed it in BEFORE the deadline.

We all started to panic and talk at once.

Sasha raised her hand, signaling us to quiet down. "Listen, people, I'm sorry, but the rules are the rules!"

"I don't understand," I said. "I filled out the form and turned it in myself. How can we be disqualified?!" I was on the verge of tears.

"Yeah, it WAS turned in on time," she answered. "The problem is that it's INCOMPLETE! It doesn't say on here that the name of your group is Dorkalicious."

She handed the entry form to me, and everyone crowded around to read it for themselves.

In the blank where it said "Name of act," I had scrawled, "Actually, I'm not really sure yet."

My heart sank! Everyone shook their heads in shock and disbelief.

I crumpled the entry form and jammed it into my pocket as tears flooded my eyes. "I am SO sorry, guys!" I muttered. "I guess she's right. It's all my fault. I don't know what to say. . . ."

"I CAN'T believe it!" Violet exclaimed. "Nikki, how could you forget to do something so important?"

I just shrugged my shoulders and stared at the floor.

That's when Brandon came to my defense.

"Well, we have to remember that this whole band thing was kind of thrown together at the last minute. We hadn't even picked a name yet."

Sasha started talking into a headset, and suddenly the house lights dimmed.

The curtains opened to reveal the first act, which was a seventh-grade rap group dressed in fuzzy dog costumes. They were performing the song "Who Let the Dogs Out?"

I hoped it was supposed to be a comedy act.

"This is SO unfair!" Chloe groaned.

"There has to be something we can do!" Zoey moaned.

"That's showbiz!" Violet said sarcastically.

Sasha shot us a dirty look and covered the mic on her headset. "In case you haven't

noticed, I'm trying to put on a show here.
Take it out in the hall. Please!"

We sighed and slowly shuffled out of the
dark auditorium. Then the five of us threw
a private pity party for Dorkalicious.

Everyone looked SO disappointed. It was heartbreaking.

I could NOT believe I had let them all down like that.

I was the most horrible friend EVER!

I didn't know what to say, so I just apologized again.

"Guys, I'm REALLY, REALLY sorry. I can't believe we won't be performing after all those long hours of practice. I wish there was a way to make this up to you. . . ."

Everyone gave me a small smile and shrugged it off.

"Hey, so what! They only kicked us out of the talent show! It's NOT the end of the world," Chloe said, smiling goofily and doing her jazz hands.

"And with the Dragon Lady running things, there's no way we're getting backstage to take down our equipment," Theodore said. "I'm outta here! Pizza, anyone?"

"Yeah, we can always get our stuff after the show tomorrow," Marcus added. "Pizza sounds GREAT to me!"

Everyone started to cheer up a bit and agreed to hang out at the pizza place across the street. Which was a good idea since our parents weren't scheduled to pick us up from practice for another two hours.

But I still felt horrible and my stomach was churning. Just the thought of pizza made me feel ill.

"Sorry, guys, but I'm exhausted. I think I'm gonna head home."

"Come on, Nikki, don't beat yourself up!" Brandon pleaded.

"Yeah, we gave it our best shot!" Violet added.

"But more than anything, we had fun hanging out and practicing together, right?!" Chloe said, giving me a hug.

"I guess so. Listen, you guys go ahead. I'm gonna call it a night, 'kay? Eat a piece of pizza for me," I said, smiling weakly.

Finally they gave up trying to talk me into going with them.

Even though everyone was disappointed by our disqualification, they were trying to be good sports about it.

I do NOT deserve friends like these!

I could hear them laughing and joking as they headed out the front door.

I found a pay phone and called home for a ride. As I sat at the front door waiting for my mom to arrive, I started to feel even worse.

Winning a talent show scholarship was my only hope for staying at WCD.

And now even that is gone.

I buried my face in my knees and cried.

Suddenly I heard footsteps approaching.

I quickly brushed away my tears and wiped my runny nose on my sleeve.

"Nikki, you look horrible!" MacKenzie said, sneering. "OMG! What kind of lip gloss are you wearing? Oh, that's not lip gloss . . . it's SNOT!"

I was like, JUST GREAT! I rolled my eyes at her.

"I heard Dorkalicious got disqualified. Too bad! Thank goodness Jessica has office duty during fourth hour and was able to check your entry form to make sure you weren't cheating."

"MacKenzie, I wasn't trying to cheat. We just hadn't selected a name yet. . . ."

"Well, look at the good side! At least now you won't have to get up onstage and publicly humiliate yourself. AGAIN! And with both Dorkalicious AND SuperFreaks out of the way, it will be an easy win for me and my dancers!"

"MacKenzie, you are a dismally vain, self-absorbed blond abyss of seething wretchedness!" I blurted out.

She smiled at me wickedly. "You say that like it's a BAD thing!"

Then she took out her lip gloss and slathered on a fresh layer.

"Anyway, I didn't come out here to talk to YOU. Now that Brandon is no longer in

329

the talent show, Sasha needs him to handle the photography."

"Unfortunately, he left a few minutes ago."

MacKenzie eyed me carefully, trying to figure out if I was lying or not.

"Well, if you see him, please give him the message that Sasha and I need to talk to him."

"Since when am I your personal secretary? If you have a message for Brandon, you can tell him yourself."

MacKenzie placed her hands on her hips and flashed another evil smile. "Crush much? Get a clue, hon. You want Brandon? Dial 1-800-YOU-WISH!!" Then she spun around and sashayed down the hall.

I just HATE it when MacKenzie sashays.

Just then my mom pulled up, and I dragged myself out to the car.

"So, practice got out early?" she asked.

"Yeah, something like that," I mumbled.

As soon as I got home, I rushed up to my room and collapsed on my bed.

I just lay there in the darkness, pondering my massively cruddy situation.

I am SUCH a LOSER!

And a PATHETIC friend!

I want to believe that things are so bad, they can't get any worse.

But I already know it's going to get worse.

A LOT worse!

Tomorrow morning I am going to have to tell my parents the truth about EVERYTHING! ☹!!

SATURDAY, NOVEMBER 30

When I finally woke up, it was almost noon.

Knowing that I was going to have to face my parents made me feel a little nauseated.

On top of that, the sun was shining in my eyes and I had a splitting headache.

I was surprised to see that I still had on my clothes from last night. I grabbed my pillow, groaned, and buried my head under it.

Suddenly there was a knock on my door. But I ignored it.

Most Saturday mornings, Brianna and Miss Penelope wake me up. But today was my lucky day.

Before I could yell "GO AWAY!" Brianna, Miss Penelope, AND my grandma all barged in.

A TRIPLE dose of INSANITY could easily destroy the very weak grip I held on my pathetic reality.

It was enough to make me want to jump out of my bedroom window screaming.

"Wake up! Wake up!" Brianna screamed. "Me, Grandma, and Miss Penelope need you to help us make some homemade ice cream!"

My grandma sat next to me on the bed and tickled me. "Time to get up, Miss Lazy Bones!"

"Please, Grandma. Stop! I don't feel so good! And I'm exhausted!"

"Well, no wonder. How can you get a good night's sleep with all this junk on your bed? Backpack, book, sneakers, and . . . ?"

She picked up a crumpled piece of paper that had fallen out of my pocket.

". . . assorted litter. Is this any good, or can I throw it away?" she said, opening it up and reading it. She slid her glasses down her nose a bit and squinted.

"Oh, THAT thing. It's nothing. Just toss it!" I muttered.

I shoved my head back under the pillow, hoping Grandma and Brianna would take the hint and get lost.

"Are you sure, honey? This looks like it might be important. Hmmm? WCD Talent Showcase Entry Form. So, the name of your band is Actually, I'm Not Really Sure Yet. Now, that's a bit odd, don't cha think?"

"Miss Penelope says she's looking for chocolate cupcakes. Any cupcakes in here, Nikki?!" Brianna said as she rummaged through my sock drawer.

That's when I peeked out from under my pillow.

"NO, Brianna! There are no cupcakes inside my sock drawer. And Grandma, NO! That's NOT the name of my band! Like, how totally STUPID would that —"

I stopped midsentence.

Inside my head, my brain was screaming, "OMG! OMG! THAT'S IT!!"

I'd just gotten the most FANTASTIC idea!

Maybe there was still hope for our band after all.

I was so happy, I hugged Grandma.

"I LOVE YOU, GRANDMA!" I giggled as I jumped up and down on my bed.

She climbed up and joined me. "I love you, too, sweetheart! I'm glad you're feeling better."

"Hey! What about MEEEEEE?!" Brianna screeched. "And Miss Penelope. We wanna jump too!"

All four of us held hands and jumped on my bed like it was a trampoline or something.

I promised to help make the ice cream as soon as I'd made a few phone calls.

So Grandma and Brianna rushed downstairs singing "Girls Just Want to Have Fun" at the top of their lungs and really off-key.

I could hardly wait to call Chloe and Zoey.

When I told them my idea for getting us back into the talent show, they thought it was brilliant.

Next we called Violet, Brandon, Theodore, and Marcus and made plans to meet with Sasha to update her about our new status.

My final task was to make some major design adjustments to our band T-shirts.

Later that evening everything went as planned and we cornered Sasha backstage.

I smoothed out our crumpled entry form as best I could and handed it back to her.

However, before Sasha could read it, MacKenzie came rushing over. "Nikki Maxwell, WHAT are you doing here? Sasha has already told you Dorkalicious is disqualified!"

"MacKenzie, we're not entering the talent show as Dorkalicious," I said happily. "Our entry form is correct."

MacKenzie looked totally confused. "WHAT?! If you're not Dorkalicious, then who are you?!"

She obviously didn't have a clue.

Sasha read over our entry form and slowly nodded. "Yeah, it makes sense. If that's the name of your band, I guess you guys are back in the show. . . ."

"WHAT! How can they be back in the show? Nikki, you can't get away with this!" MacKenzie screamed, stomping her foot like a toddler having a temper tantrum or something. "It's not FAIR!!"

"Later, MacKenzie!" I said. "Break a leg!"

Only I REALLY meant it.

Well, okay. I meant it just a little.

The word got around quickly that we were back in and that the competition was going to be brutal.

After the show started, we sat in a dressing room watching all the other acts on a television monitor.

There were magic acts, dance groups, bands, singers, and musicians, and most of them were really good.

Winning the talent show was NOT going to be easy.

After about an hour and a half the assistant stage manager finally took us backstage and told us to wait in the wings since we were going next.

MacKenzie's dance group was performing, and I had to admit they were awesome.

They wore sequined jumpsuits and pretty much danced their butts off to a medley of the latest pop tunes.

The crowd went wild.

Since our band was added to the lineup at the last minute, we were the last act to go.

Violet and the guys were entering from stage left, and Chloe, Zoey, and I were entering from stage right.

While we were waiting to go on, suddenly my stomach started doing double somersaults.

I must have been having a panic attack or something because my brain was screaming stuff like, "WHAT are YOU doing?! You CAN'T go out there and sing in front of all those people! What if you MESS UP?! Your life will be RUINED!!"

But I wanted that scholarship so badly that I didn't have a choice.

Chloe and Zoey must have sensed my fear because they each took my hand and squeezed it and told me I was going to do fine.

My knees still felt really wobbly. But it was great to know that if they actually gave out and I fell over, Chloe and Zoey would be there to drag me across the stage and stick the microphone in my hand.

They are, like, the BEST friends EVER!

I cannot begin to explain what it felt like to hear the crowd when the announcer introduced us. . . .

"And our next act is a band made up of Nikki, Chloe, Zoey, Brandon, Violet, Theodore, and Marcus. Please welcome to the stage . . .

ACTUALLY, I'M NOT REALLY SURE YET!!"

I really LOVED our new name! It sounded edgy and professional, just like those real bands on MTV!

We quickly walked onstage and took our places.

I nervously glanced out at the audience and squinted, trying to spot faces I knew. But due to the glare of the bright stage lights, the crowd was just a big massive blur of darkness, noise, and excitement.

Which actually was a good thing, because not seeing a million people staring back at me made me feel less nervous.

I looked over my shoulder, and Brandon gave me a huge smile and a thumbs-up.

He then did four taps with his drumsticks, launching Violet, Theodore, and Marcus into the intro of the song.

OMG! They sounded SO good! I had to remind myself it was my four friends playing that music live, and NOT a song blasting on my iPod.

Chloe, Zoey, and I started our dance routine just the way we had practiced it.

Then I smiled at my BFFs, took a deep breath, and sang the first note.

At first it felt a little shocking to hear my own voice so loud and clear. But I just tried to relax and enjoy our performance.

By the time we got to the chorus . . .

"Dork, nerd, geek, freak
Is all you see
But just back off
And let me be ME!"

. . . I could see the first two rows had gotten up on their feet and were dancing along.

When we finally finished our song, the crowd cheered like crazy and we got a standing ovation.

They actually loved us!

Chloe, Zoey, and I hugged one another as our musicians exchanged fist bumps and high fives.

I was SO hoping we were going to win. We HAD to win!!

All the acts quickly filed back onstage and lined up around us.

As MacKenzie and her dance group crowded in right next to us, she smiled sweetly at Brandon. "You guys were awesome! Good luck!"

"Thanks! Good luck to you, too!" he said politely.

Then MacKenzie turned and looked at me like I was something she had scraped off the bottom of her shoe.

Which didn't surprise me one bit.

As the judge, Mr. Trevor Chase, took the stage, the tension was so thick you could cut it with a knife.

"As you are aware, ALL the talent here was very, very good. I encourage each of you to continue to hone your craft. But tonight there can only be one winner. And the winner . . ."

I held my breath and chanted inside my head, Please let it be us. Please let it be us. Please let it be us!

". . . of the tenth annual WCD Talent Showcase is . . . Mac's Maniacs!"

MacKenzie shrieked! Then she hugged Jessica as all her dancers crowded around hugging one another.

I was SO disappointed, I felt like crying.

It wasn't the losing part that made me feel so bad, but the fact that I was going to have to leave WCD and my friends.

I think the rest of my band was a bit surprised we lost, but they were being really good sports about it.

After we left the stage, we all hugged one another too. And everyone told me I sang really well.

"Nikki, this was SO fun!" Violet gushed. "We didn't win. But, hey, that's . . ."

"SHOWBIZ!" all seven of us shouted, and then erupted into peals of laughter at our little joke.

But deep down inside, I felt really horrible knowing I was going to have to say good-bye to everyone in a few days.

My eyes started to tear up, but I didn't want my friends to see me crying.

"Um, my throat is a little dry. I'm gonna run out to the hall to get a drink. I'll be right back, 'kay?" I announced, and took off before anyone had a chance to join me.

I went straight to the girls' bathroom and splashed water on my face. I cringed at the thought of having to tell my parents all the crazy stuff I'd done.

Suddenly the bathroom door opened and MacKenzie rudely brushed past me in a hurry.

"Excuse you!" she hissed as she whipped out her makeup. "I have a photo shoot to do."

I just rolled my eyes at her.

"Too bad you lost! I tried to warn you not to waste your time. At least Jessica and

I will FINALLY get to have lockers next to each other when YOU transfer to a public school! Ever since your dad got hired as the exterminator, our school has been overrun with bugs.

"Besides, you're way too poor to pay that tuition bill that you got in the mail last week, so you —" MacKenzie got this really funny look on her face and bit her lip. Then she took out her lip gloss and nervously slathered on a thick layer.

I wanted to tell her to keep her nose out of my business and that she had no idea what she was talking about. Although, to be honest, she knew EXACTLY what she was talking about because there was no WAY we could pay that tuition bill and —

Suddenly it hit me. MacKenzie did know EXACTLY what she was talking about, but HOW was that possible? How did she know about my bill, and why was she now squirming and avoiding eye contact?

I put my hands on my hips and stared right into her beady little eyes. "So, MacKenzie . . . HOW did you know I got a tuition bill? Or did your BFF Jessica also send YOU a copy of the PHONY BILL that she sent ME?!"

"Well, she's just the fifth-hour office assistant. She would NEVER, like, mail out stuff to people, actually . . ." MacKenzie stumbled as her cheeks flushed.

I could not believe my ears. For the past two weeks my life had pretty much been one gigantic, continuous nightmare as I desperately tried to figure out how to pay that tuition bill.

Then I'd practically had a meltdown dealing with the mental anguish of a possible transfer to a new school.

ONLY to FINALLY find out it was just another of MacKenzie's cruel pranks??!!

Right then I was SO angry I wanted to grab one of MacKenzie's $495 suede Prada ballet flats and shove it right down her throat. I took a step toward her.

"YOU and Jessica sent me a phony tuition bill?! I've been worried sick about how my parents were going to pay it. How could you do that?!"

MacKenzie nervously batted her eyes at her perfect reflection in the mirror and then snapped the cap back on her lip gloss.

"I don't have the slightest idea what you're talking about."

"MacKenzie, you are such a liar!"

"And besides, even if we DID send you a phony tuition bill, you don't have any proof! Do you? . . . LOSER!!"

With that, she turned and sashayed out of the bathroom.

I just HATE it when MacKenzie sashays!

Although, to be honest, I was SUPER-relieved to find out that bill was from HER and NOT the school.

I felt like I was finally waking up from a two-week-long nightmare.

Well, I learned my lesson, that's for sure!

No more secrets! I was going to tell Chloe and Zoey about my dad and my scholar-ship the first chance I got.

And once the entire school knew about it, I would no longer have to lie awake nights wondering if and when MacKenzie was going to drop the bomb.

It was like a heavy weight was lifting off my shoulders even as I thought about it.

Just then Chloe and Zoey rushed into the bathroom out of breath.

"Oh, there you are! We've been looking everywhere for you!" Zoey panted. "MacKenzie told us you were in here."

"OMG! You are NOT going to believe what just happened!" Chloe's eyes were huge!

"After you left," Zoey continued, "Trevor Chase came over and congratulated us. He said he wanted to let us know that *15 Minutes of Fame* features unpolished amateurs going through boot camp to get better. He said we sounded really professional and were actually too good to be on his show. Can you believe THAT?! He said he won't start filming the new season until next fall, and that's when MacKenzie's group will get to audition. But he wants to work with us RIGHT NOW! Nikki, he LOVED our song and wants us to release it ASAP!"

"WHAT! Are you kidding?! NO WAY!" I sputtered.

"Yep! He says he wants to meet with all of us and our parents after the holidays and that he'll be in touch!" Chloe continued.

The three of us started screaming and did a group hug!

I could NOT believe that people all over the world might actually be able to hear OUR song!

And if we made any money, I could use MY portion to FINALLY buy myself a CELL PHONE ☺!!

Back in the auditorium, I was talking to my parents when Principal Winston came up and congratulated me.

I was praying that he wouldn't mention that bug extermination fiasco.

But he did!

Apparently, my parents had run into Principal Winston and his wife at that restaurant last Sunday. He and Dad had chatted and then arranged a meeting for next Saturday to evaluate the WCD bug problem.

Thank goodness my dad had NOT gotten fired after all. I was SO relieved!

I never thought in a million years I'd actually be happy he was the WCD exterminator.

But more than anything, I'm SUPER-grateful that Dad arranged my scholarship. I guess I didn't really appreciate it until I thought I had lost it.

Anyway, I already know the ONLY bugs Dad and Principal Winston are going to find at WCD are in a jar in MacKenzie's locker.

But I've learned my lesson the hard way, courtesy of MacKenzie.

I will NEVER, EVER stick my nose in my dad's business again! And that's a PROMISE!

So I just kept my big mouth shut about the WCD bugs.

After we'd changed out of our band T-shirts, Chloe, Zoey, and Violet went back to the dressing rooms to pack up the rest of our stuff.

Brandon and I sat in the second row of the auditorium, which was now pretty much empty.

He told me that renaming our band Actually, I'm Not Really Sure Yet at the last moment was pure genius.

But I admitted that it was my grandma who had given me the idea.

He also said he was really proud of me and that I was such a good singer, I could be a star.

I was like, yeah right, a not-so-talented pop star!

So, we were just sitting there facing each other, and he kind of stared at me for what seemed like FOREVER.

I blushed and my stomach got all fluttery inside.

OMG! I just HATE it when he does that to me.

Then I smiled. And he smiled back at me with this sort of shy look on his face.

I almost FREAKED when Brandon kind of leaned forward a little until we were, like, three inches apart.

My heart was pounding so hard I could hear it in my ears.

Because for a second I thought that maybe he was going to . . . you know . . . !!!

SQUEEEEEEEEEEE ☺!!!

But that's when Brianna suddenly popped up from the row right behind us and leaned over our seats and shoved her fist right in Brandon's face and shouted:

"WHAT'S UP, DUDE? MEET MISS PENELOPE! SHE WAS BORNED FROM A PEN! AND SHE SAYS YOU HAVE COOTIES!!"

I could NOT believe Brianna actually did that.

OMG! I was SO embarrassed.

But mostly I felt SUPERGIGGLY and INSANELY HAPPY because everything had worked out.

So I grabbed Miss Penelope and gave her a big, fat, sloppy kiss.

SMACK!!

Which totally grossed her out.

"Her" being Brianna, not Miss Penelope.

And of course Brandon and I both cracked up.

I guess he knows by now that I'm just weird like that.

OMG!

I am SUCH a DORK!!

☺!!

ABOUT THE AUTHOR

Rachel Renée Russell is the #1 *New York Times* bestselling author of the blockbuster book series Dork Diaries and the exciting new series The Misadventures of Max Crumbly.

There are more than forty-five million copies of her books in print worldwide, and they have been translated into thirty-six languages.

She enjoys working with her daughter Nikki who helps illustrate her books.

Rachel's message is "Always let your inner dork shine through!"

The employees of Thorndike Press hope you have enjoyed this Large Print book. All our Thorndike, Wheeler, and Kennebec Large Print titles are designed for easy reading, and all our books are made to last. Other Thorndike Press Large Print books are available at your library, through selected bookstores, or directly from us.

For information about titles, please call:
(800) 223-1244

or visit our website at:
http://gale.cengage.com/thorndike

To share your comments, please write:
Publisher
Thorndike Press
10 Water St., Suite 310
Waterville, ME 04901